'I Want You,

'And you're goir...
I've already invit...

'For what?' she asked wearily.

'For *you*, body and soul. I want your quick mind, your sudden flashes of temper and the way you try to read what I'm thinking, with your eyes thoughtful and dark. I want to hear your voice and touch your hair. I want your hand in mine, and your mouth on my mouth. I want every last bit of your being. I want it all!'

'But Tristan, the price of that . . . is *marriage*.'

LAUREY BRIGHT

discovered the magic of reading early in life, and hopes that her books will bring that same magic to others. Although her interests are varied, including history and ecology, she first began writing love stories at sixteen, and has never wanted to be anything but a writer.

Dear Reader:

Silhouette Books is pleased to announce the creation of a new line of contemporary romances—*Silhouette Special Editions*. Each month we'll bring you six new love stories written by the best of today's authors—Janet Dailey, Brooke Hastings, Laura Hardy, Sondra Stanford, Linda Shaw, Patti Beckman, and many others.

Silhouette Special Editions are written with American women in mind; they are for readers who want more: more story, more details and descriptions, more realism, and more *romance*. *Special Editions* are longer than most contemporary romances allowing for a closer look at the relationship between hero and heroine with emphasis on heightened romantic tension and greater sensuous and sensual detail. If you want more from a romance, be sure to look for *Silhouette Special Editions* on sale this February wherever you buy books.

We welcome any suggestions or comments, and I invite you to write us at the address below.

Karen Solem
Editor-in-Chief
Silhouette Books
P.O. Box 769
New York, N. Y. 10019

LAUREY BRIGHT
Sweet Vengeance

Silhouette Romance

Published by Silhouette Books New York

America's Publisher of Contemporary Romance

Other Silhouette Books by Laurey Bright

Tears of Morning

SILHOUETTE BOOKS, a Simon & Schuster Division of
GULF & WESTERN CORPORATION
1230 Avenue of the Americas, New York, N.Y. 10020

ISBN: 0-671-57125-7

First Silhouette Books printing January, 1982

10 9 8 7 6 5 4 3 2 1

Map by Tony Ferrara

America's Publisher of Contemporary Romance

Printed in the U.S.A.

Sweet
Vengeance

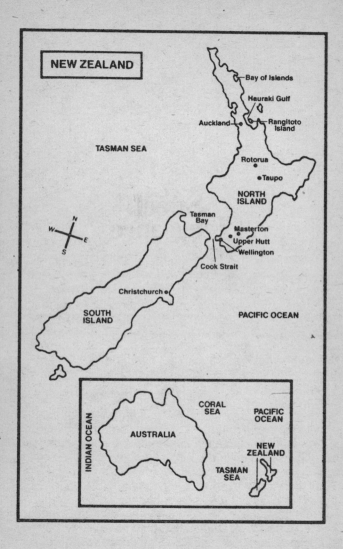

Chapter One

The day was almost suffocatingly hot, the heat rising in visible waves from the pavement on Queen Street, the sun glittering harshly on the blue-green ripples of the Waitemáta Harbour as Larissa made her way to downtown Auckland. The sea could be glimpsed in tantalising flashes between the tall buildings that had risen almost at the water's edge, and ships were anchored only yards from the traffic that swept noisily along from the Harbour Bridge into the city. There must be a cruise ship in, she thought idly. She recognised the slow, attractive North American drawl of a couple admiring a shop window filled with paua-shell jewellery, and had to dodge to avoid a camera being swung carelessly by a Japanese matron chattering incomprehensibly to her husband, who wore a tropical suit of a startling patterned material and a broad white straw hat.

Larissa turned the corner and made her way to the big modern hotel that was her objective. She supposed there would be air conditioning; wiping fine beads of sweat from her upper lip with her forefinger, she blessed the marvels of modern technology. Hitching up her capacious leather bag as it threatened to slip off the shoulder of her cool, silky sleeveless blouse, she pushed open the hotel door and thankfully stepped into the wide tiled lobby.

As she approached the reception desk and the politely smiling girl behind it she glanced at the slip of paper she had taken from her bag. 'Mr.—Ashley Morris is expecting me,' she said.

The girl didn't stop smiling, but a flicker of speculation in her eyes made Larissa add hastily, 'I'm from the Stenserve Secretarial Agency. He asked for a shorthand-typist.'

The girl gave her the room number, and the lift wafted her up several floors. She stepped out, and a lush, heavily patterned thick pile carpet deadened the sound of her footsteps as she counted the numbers on the doors and knocked firmly when she came to the right one.

The man who opened the door was stocky and fair, and he barely waited for her to show him the card with the agency's name on it before he interrupted her murmured, 'Mr. Morris? I'm from Stenserve—' and waved her into the room.

'Good, good!' he said heartily. 'Come in, we've been expecting you—'

It was scarcely twenty minutes since he had phoned the agency, but she said politely, 'I hope I haven't kept you waiting?'

He said something in reply, but she scarcely heard him. As she moved into the room, taking in the spaciousness of it, the large table by the window littered with papers and with a typewriter at one end of it, and the rumpled bed where evidently someone had been sitting, with more papers over its surface, she saw the other man who stood at the window with his back to her, looking out over the harbour. He wore a crisply ironed white shirt with the sleeves rolled up to the elbow, and dark pants that hugged lean hips and long legs, one hand thrust into a pocket and the other behind his neck. Lean fingers kneaded slightly at taut skin below sleek pale hair as he flung his head back a little and lifted straight shoulders in a gesture of relief from strain.

It was a gesture she knew well, and it stopped her in her tracks for several seconds, while Mr. Morris said something about contracts and signatures and notes and typing. It was useless to tell herself that lots of men looked alike from the back, that there had been countless times when the way a man walked or held his head, the cut of his hair, the breadth of his shoulders, had briefly fooled her. She knew the moment she saw those long fingers where once hers had sometimes rested and caressed, that the inevitable had finally happened. That when he turned at last and faced her, she was going to be looking at the man she had hoped never to see again. Tristan. Tristan Sharpe.

Mr. Morris's flow of talk had abated, and he was waving her to a leather-covered chair and asking politely for her name. She stood by the chair and watched Tristan's back as she said clearly, 'Larissa Lovegrove, Mr. Morris.'

The white shirt remained smooth across the taut shoulders. The kneading hand left the area above his collar, not suddenly, but with calm and apparently casual slowness. For a moment he remained contemplating the view, and then he turned and her heart seemed to alter its rhythm a little as she stared into well-remembered cool blue eyes, analytical and appraising and without surprise or embarrassment.

His glance encompassed her dark hair, not falling about her shoulders with unruly curling ends as he must remember it, but combed back sleekly and pinned high, emphasising the slight tilt of her brown eyes and giving her face, which was thinner than it had been, a faintly oriental distinction; then his eyes lingered briefly on her lips, firmly closed to cover her clenched teeth, slid quickly over the curve of her high breasts under the thin blouse and the slenderness of her waist, and took in the slim, fashionable skirt and the lightly tanned bare legs before returning to her face.

He said, 'Hallo, Larissa.' His voice was even and deep; there was just the slightest hint in it of the faintly mocking pronunciation he had used when he first began to call her by her given name, and perhaps that was why she reacted by saying, 'Hello, Mr. Sharpe.'

His straight brows rose just a little, and his mouth moved in a small, sardonic grimace. It wasn't a mouth that smiled often, and although there was an austere masculine beauty in its outline, it was at best inclined to appear uncompromising, and at worst downright cruel. The impression was reinforced by his nose, which was a shade long and in profile had a tendency to look intimidating.

Mr. Morris was smiling delightedly, saying, 'You two know each other?'

'Yes,' Tristan said easily. 'We used to work together years ago.'

'Mr. Sharpe means I used to work for him,' Larissa said, seating herself in the chair and lowering her head to open the bag on her lap. That way she didn't have to look at him—at either of them. By the time she had taken out her notebook and pencil, she could glance up with a cool professional smile, saying, 'I'm ready. What would you like me to do?'

It was to do with a contract, she gathered. Her typing skills were the main requirement, but there were notes to be taken and transcribed, too. Mr. Morris was an Australian and had flown over the Tasman to finalise the details of what she gathered was a kind of takeover by Tristan's firm. She concentrated on what she was doing quite fiercely so that she shouldn't be so aware of Tristan's presence in the room, of his quiet, even voice as he spoke to the other man and occasionally gave her an instruction or confirmed a suggestion of Mr. Morris's.

When it was all over and she had made several copies of the contract to be checked over by their respective lawyers, it was late and she felt wrung out. Mr. Morris looked flushed and pleased with himself, and said something about looking forward to an early retirement and a trip round the world with the missus. And Tristan looked just as always, self-contained, confident, and not giving a thing away.

Mr. Morris insisted on giving her dinner, and although she tried to refuse, she found herself going into the hotel dining room with the two men, not quite sure why she hadn't been firm in her refusal, unless it was because Tristan's silence on the subject had needled her. Surely he could at least have indicated his willingness to have her with them, if only for politeness? She wondered somewhat angrily if his silence meant indifference, or a positive aversion to her company. Glancing at his face, she saw it was coldly neutral, and was assailed by a strong desire to get under his skin, to make him drop the mask and show some emotion. While he forked into a ham salad, and she toyed with a seafood cocktail, she eyed him covertly, remembering with a bitter detachment the way he had once roused her to a fever of confused emotions, quite deliberately and without ever losing his own cold self-command—except, she reminded herself, perhaps once. And even that might have been pretence, a calculated move in the complicated relationship that had developed between them. He had always been two jumps ahead of her, right to the end, an end which she had brought about with a clumsiness and lack of finesse which had shamed her but had been crudely effective. She had been too young to do it as it should

11

have been done, with decency and a sophistication to match his, too young to even comprehend fully why it was imperative that she break free of him, with no possibility of return. Too young to attempt to pierce the armour of the icy personality that he showed the world and find out what lay beneath it. She had only known that he both fascinated and frightened her, and in the end it was the fear that led her finally to break the fatal spell of his attraction.

It hadn't been easy, afterwards, to make a life without him. She hadn't realised how much he had taken over and filled her life, influenced her hopes and plans. There had been moments when the fierce ache of longing had almost overwhelmed her, and other times when she desperately wished he was there with his astringent advice and detached brand of protection. But gradually she had found her feet again and learned to function without him. She had got herself another job, saved some money, gone overseas, even learned to handle a light love affair without intensity or deep undercurrents, and without dramatics when the man moved on, perhaps to some other woman who might be more willing to progress beyond the limits Larissa imposed on their lovemaking.

He looked up as he pushed aside his plate and found her eyes on him. His face remained almost expressionless, and she was washed with sudden irritation. She was older now, and a good deal more knowledgeable than she had been five years ago. And not afraid any more. It had been borne in on her in recent years that she was attractive to men, good to look at and with a certain mysterious womanly power that drew men to her, though most of them were rebuffed. Tristan had once paid her the supreme compliment of wanting to make her his wife, and now he looked at her with apparently total indifference. Curiosity and pique stirred in her. She had never exactly understood why he had wanted her, unless it was the attraction of opposites. She had been young and passionate and hopelessly inexperienced, with nothing but a good brain and a passably pretty face to set against his brilliance with figures and finance, his knowledge of a hundred subjects whose surfaces she had only begun to scratch, his stern good looks and occasional unexpected flashes of satiric charm, and his undoubted experience.

It had been no contest, then, but she was no longer a girl, no longer easily frightened—or fascinated. She returned his cool stare with a calm look of her own and didn't drop her eyes, and for a moment a flicker of some expression she couldn't read made his gaze a fraction less cool, less impersonal, before he turned in response to a remark from the other man. He scarcely looked at her again until the meal was over, and then to her surprise he offered to run her home.

'That isn't necessary,' she said. 'My fare will be included in the agency's bill.'

'I'll take you,' he said quietly, but his hand on her arm was bruising as he steered her out of the dining room. Ashley Morris was loudly giving his approval to the idea, shaking hands with them both and thanking her profusely for her services.

Tristan didn't let go her arm until he opened the door of a discreetly expensive-looking car in the hotel's basement carpark and put her firmly into it.

She wondered if he knew his own strength, and surreptitiously rubbed her arm with the fingers of her other hand as he went round to the driver's seat. He wasn't a burly man, and he moved with a lithe masculine grace so that one didn't notice the width of his shoulders or the latent power in his hands. He might spend most of his working days behind a desk, but she knew that he was a keen yachtsman who had taken part in some of the most gruelling ocean races in the Pacific area, and that he played a mean game of squash.

She dropped her hand to curve it about the top of her bag as he slid in beside her.

'Where to?' he asked her.

'Pakuranga.' She directed him through the city to the pleasant eastern suburb with its hills covered with neat homes on quarter-acre sections filled with flourishing trees and pretty gardens, until he stopped outside the block of flats where she lived in the rear unit of three. They had scarcely spoken in the twenty minutes it took to make the journey, and she said 'Thank you' stiffly and made to get out.

As her hand found the unfamiliar doorlatch and tried to manipulate it, he said, 'Aren't you going to invite me in?'

She sat very still for a moment, and then turned. 'Do you want to come in?' she asked, a faint challenge in her tone.

'Yes.'

He didn't add anything to the flat monosyllable, and his voice told her nothing. She knew his expression would be equally uninformative, though it was growing rapidly darker now, and she couldn't see his face very well.

'All right,' she said. 'If you like,'

He got out and opened her door for her, and she led the way up the path beneath an overshadowing jacaranda, its faded purple blossoms littering the narrow strip of concrete and the neatly trimmed grass border.

Tristan looked up at the arch of the branches and said, 'It's a bit big for the space, isn't it?'

'I suppose so,' she said shortly. 'But we like it.' The tenants of the three flats all nurtured their tree, and didn't mind trimming it when it threatened to get out of hand, or picking up the spent flowers when they fell. While it bloomed it was breathtakingly beautiful, and all summer it made a welcome patch of lace-patterned shade on the lawn.

She unlocked the door and switched on the light in the small living room, putting down her bag on one of the pair of small matching kauri tables she had picked up in a junk shop and restored. The room was furnished in creams and golds with touches of jewel-bright colours in huge cushions she had made herself to serve in the place of chairs. The beige carpet and cream striped wallpaper had come with the flat, but her own personality was imprinted on the rest of the décor. She motioned Tristan to sit on the long, deep sofa and said, 'Can I give you a drink?' There was a room divider which screened off the small kitchen, and on the living-room side, under the counter, she kept a shelf of wines and spirits. She made to move towards it, but he said, 'No thanks. Come here and sit down.'

She hesitated, and he said, softly, 'I'm not planning to rape you, Larissa.'

'No,' she said. 'You're not the type, are you?'

His eyebrows rose a little, and he said, 'Do I detect a note of disappointment?'

Larissa flared, 'You always had a nasty brand of sarcastic humour.'

'I'm sorry,' he said, sounding more amused than contrite. '*You* haven't changed much, either,'

'I have!' she said emphatically. He meant she was quick-tempered, she supposed. He had never known that it was only he who made her so. He had rocked her off balance from the start, aroused all kinds of emotions she hadn't known she possessed, and anger was just one of them. And she had only regained her equilibrium when she at last found the courage to drastically cut herself free of his domination. With something like dismay she recognised the familiarity of an old pattern in this exchange, her own sharp antagonism and his coolly amused reaction; just like old times, she thought bitterly.

But it wasn't going to be like that. Five years of water under a lot of bridges had surely cured her of girlish tantrums and taught her a thing or two about men and how to handle them, even the most obnoxious of them.

With an effort she suppressed her resentment and assumed a polite, distant half smile. 'It's been a long time,' she said conversationally, seating herself gracefully on the other end of the sofa and twisting her body a little to face him.

'Yes,' he agreed suavely. 'Hasn't it?' The mockery was stronger now, deriding her safe conversational gambit, but she maintained her poise and when he said, 'And what have you been doing with yourself these last five years?' she took the remark at face value and told him. Six months as secretary to a television producer, a couple of years in England, with continental holidays thrown in, a stint in an advertising agency in Australia, and home to New Zealand where she had been working for a year now as a temporary secretary for the agency, being sent to different short-term jobs around the city.

'Do you enjoy it?' he asked.

'Yes. I like variety.'

'I remember.'

She didn't know if that was meant as a jibe, intended to sting. His face didn't alter as he said it. There was a short, strained silence, and she said, injecting lightness into her voice, 'And you? What have you been doing? Making more money?'

'Among other things.'

She wondered suddenly if he was married. He must be nearly thirty-four. He might have acquired a wife and several children by now. There had always been plenty of women who would have jumped at the chance.

'What other things?' she asked him. 'I suppose you're married?'

'Then you suppose wrongly,' he said curtly. His eyes sharpened a little and she knew he was studying her for her reaction. 'If I was,' he said, 'I wouldn't be here with you.'

They were just sitting there talking, with at least three feet of space between them. Acting the sophisticate, she raised her brows in a parody of his own habitual mocking manner and said, 'Dear me, you *are* strait-laced, aren't you? What on earth could your wife possibly object to, supposing you had one? There's absolutely nothing—'

'—yet,' he said, stopping her as her heart lurched in fright. He hadn't raised his voice but she knew there was menace in the single word, even so.

'*Ever!*' she said loudly, so that her own voice shouldn't tremble. She jumped up, started to say, 'I think you had better go—'

Tristan leaned forward a little and reached out, catching her wrist and pulling her down again, much nearer to him—far too near. He still held her wrist and his other hand was grasping her shoulder, pushing her against the back of the sofa so that she automatically threw back her head as he moved deliberately closer to her, his thigh pressing against hers, his mouth only inches from her lips.

She whispered, 'No!'

He stayed just where he was, watching her face, and she knew that her futile protest hadn't stopped him. He was terribly good at cat-and-mouse games. He would hold her just where he wanted and enjoy her frightened anticipation.

She moved her free hand, and he came closer, effectively trapping it between them. She could feel the slow, even beat of his heart against her palm. Oh, he knew what he was about all right; this wasn't even making his heartbeat quicken.

17

'Let me go!' she said icily, trying desperately to banish the panic from her eyes.

'You don't really expect me to, do you?' he asked. '*Strait-laced*, you said.'

His lips were suddenly on her throat, moving up to her ear, and the hard fingers on her shoulder smoothed over her skin to the elbow and up again, sliding to her nape to tip her head and hold it immobile as he kissed her.

'Your mistake,' he murmured, as his mouth touched hers and stopped briefly there, just touching, before he took her lips in a merciless, searing, insolently intimate way that went on and on and left her breathless and shaking when at last he lifted his head away and looked down at her.

She was shattered and unable to hide it, and she hated the cruel satisfaction in his smile.

He said suddenly, 'Do you live here alone?'

For a moment she stared back at him blankly, then her brain began to tick over, and she said quickly, 'No. No—there's someone—I have a flatmate.'

'Liar,' he said calmly.

'I'm not! It's true—'

He released her with startling abruptness and stood up, and before she had stumbled to her own feet he had flung open the door of the bedroom to inspect the small room with its single bed.

He left the door open and turned to her. 'Liar,' he repeated, and his mouth was laughing but his eyes were cold, and she shivered. As he moved towards her she took an involuntary step back. A glimmer of amusement entered his eyes, and she halted and stood her ground, her eyes meeting his defiantly.

'You said you wouldn't rape me,' she reminded him.

His brows rose in derision, so that she had an urgent desire to hit him. 'Rape?' he said, as though he had never heard of the word.

She clenched her teeth determinedly on her anger, willing herself to stay calm.

'By the way,' Tristan said, 'what happened to . . . Jeffrey, wasn't it?'

'That's none of your business!' she snapped.

He had stopped just in front of her, within touching distance, but his hands were in his pockets as he eyed her with the familiar, detached expression that she hated. 'I suppose there've been many others since then,' he said.

'That's none of your business either.'

He surveyed her in silence, his head slightly tipped to one side. 'Yes, of course there have,' he said, as though he had found the answer in her face. 'You're the girl who likes variety. I'm next.'

She nearly choked, trying to repress a gasp of shock and indignation. 'You're *nowhere!*' she managed, between her teeth. 'I *hate* you! I never want to lay eyes on you again!'

He laughed softly. 'I like your choice of words. You're going to lay eyes on me again, Larissa, my sweet. And I'm going to lay a lot more on you.'

Her cheeks burned briefly and then paled. 'You're slipping,' she said viciously. 'I don't remember you being so crude before.'

'I treated you like *glass* before!' he said with suppressed savagery. 'That was *my* mistake. I was a fool, a blind, stupid idiot. But not this time. This time I call the shots, and I know the score. This time I'm not going to put a ring on your finger, and I'm not going to be fobbed off with pretty promises and pseudo-virginal tremblings.'

'Stop it!' she said. 'Stop saying *this time!* There isn't going to be any—*anything* between you and me. That's all over!'

'Not if I know anything about it!'

'It takes two,' she said, her voice shaking. 'And you surely don't think that anything you've said just now would induce me to let you make love to me? You don't want me—you want revenge!'

His eyes slid over her with studied insult. 'Oh, I want you,' he said softly. 'I always did. Unfortunately, I didn't realise in time that you weren't the innocent maiden you pretended to be.'

'*But I was!*' she cried in desperation.

'What a ridiculous thing to say,' he observed almost dispassionately, 'in the light of what you admitted to me five years ago. Don't try that dewy-eyed act again, Larissa. It won't wash any more. And get this straight—nothing will induce me to offer you a wedding ring again. That's not part of the deal.'

'*Deal?* If this is a proposition, you're going the wrong way about it, you know!' she said furiously.

'That's exactly what it is,' he said in hard tones. 'And I want the terms clear from the start. *I'm* not a cheat.'

'For heavens sake, Tristan, neither am I! You must lis—'

But he cut in on her words. 'You won't lose by it,' he said. 'You know I have money.'

She couldn't believe that he had really said it, meant it. Stunned, she said, 'Are you offering me money—in return for—for sex?'

'My dear girl! And you said I was crude! Shall we call it simply an added inducement?' His pained tone was pure acting, and she hated him for it.

'Shall we call it payment for services rendered?' she said stingingly, more angry than she had ever been in her life but determined to retain some measure of composure. 'Would you like me to type out a contract?'

Something gleamed momentarily in his eyes, so briefly she didn't know if it was anger or something else. He said, 'What a good idea; what would you say you were worth? Or are you open to offers?'

Rage simply burst inside her, exploding into action, her hand swinging back and up in a wide, vicious arc toward his face. But he moved swiftly and caught her wrist, holding it in a painful grip so that when she scratched at his fingers with her other hand he had only to tighten his grasp fractionally to make the pain unbearable, and she had to stop fighting him. She glared at him, panting and flushed as he slanted a narrow saturnine grin at her.

'Well, you don't seem to be in the mood tonight.' He let her go slowly, his eyes wary, and she knew she had better curb the urge to attack him again because he would never let her get away with it, and he might do more than merely hold her wrist.

'One thing I will say for you, Larissa,' he said. 'You were never dull.'

'*You* were!' she said cuttingly. 'Incredibly so!'

She didn't know if the barb had found its mark. He was smiling, cynically. 'Ah, but you see, I was trying not to scare you—then,' he said. 'I must apologise for being such an unexciting lover. I think I can promise you won't be disappointed again.'

'Keep your promises!' she said stormily. 'And please get it into your conceited head that I'm not interested in you, or your money, or your rotten proposition. I might have thought, once, that I had treated you badly, that I could owe you some sort of apology, but—'

'Did you really?' he interrupted, with amused surprise, as though he hadn't thought her capable of that much integrity.

'But not any more!' she said tensely. 'Will you please go? I don't think I can stand your company any longer.'

'Something tells me I've outstayed my welcome,' he said lightly, and he stepped forward to tilt her chin with his hand. She tensed herself for the kiss she knew she couldn't avoid, every muscle rigid and unyielding as his mouth claimed dominion over hers, bruising and brief.

'Good night, Larissa,' he said, and she wanted to hit him again, because his voice was caressing, with only the faintest trace of mockery underlying the words. Her hands stayed clenched at her sides and her mouth remained as firmly closed as it had under the pressure of his lips.

His mouth quirked a little at one corner, and he left her standing there and let himself out.

She didn't begin to unwind until the sound of the car had faded to the end of the street.

He wouldn't come back, she told herself. He had simply been indulging in some virulent, twisted fun at her expense. If he had really wanted her, he wouldn't have thrown those brutal remarks at her. She would probably never see him again. Which, she told herself, was exactly what she wanted.

She was appalled and furious with herself when she recognised the painful knot in the pit of her stomach for what it was—a piercing, almost unbearable disappointment.

Chapter Two

She remembered clearly the first time she heard Tristan Sharpe's voice; she had been waiting outside his office when his secretary had gone in to announce her presence. The woman had pushed the door to, but it hadn't latched, and a slight gust of air opened it a few inches, enough for a man's voice to carry clearly to her where she stood before the secretary's desk.

'Oh, yes,' he said, sounding bored. 'And what's this one called?'

There was a rustle of paper and the muted murmur of the woman's reply, and then the man saying in a voice of unmistakable satire, 'Larissa Allegra Lovegrove! Good grief, do people really give their children names like that? Do you think she made it up in a fit of adolescent fantasy?' He didn't wait for a reply, but added almost immediately, with a return to boredom, 'Well, show her in, then. If she's anything like her name, she'll be all legs and blond curls, and no brain.'

When the secretary showed her in, Larissa was already prickling with irritation, and the cold, assessing blue stare that the man behind the big mahogany desk levelled at her as he waved her without speaking to the chair in front of it, didn't lessen her annoyance. He took in the slight flush on her cheeks and the brightness of resentment in her eyes, and she saw the quick flash of comprehension in his before it was replaced by a glint of amusement.

'Well, Miss Lovegrove,' he said. 'So you'd like to work for me?'

Perhaps she imagined the faint warning note in his voice, but it was enough to make her pause before she spoke, to swallow down the hot retort that she had no desire to work for a sarcastic brute who made fun of people's names, which were something no one could help, after all. He had no right to judge her on the strength of her name.

She hadn't thought that the job she had applied for meant working for Mr. Sharpe personally. The firm was moderately big, and expanding, and the *T. J. Sharpe* lettered on the glass of the outer door and printed in bold capitals in the newspaper advertisement she had replied to had been to her just a way of identifying the firm. If she had thought about T. J. Sharpe himself she would have imagined an aloof elderly gentleman behind a panelled door, who received clients in discreet opulence and ignored the minor minions on his staff.

Well, he was aloof, all right. Now that the glint of ironic humour had disappeared from his eyes he looked coldly impersonal and somewhat frighteningly stern, but he was far from elderly, and apparantly he had a habit of interviewing even the most unimportant prospective members of his staff himself, once his very efficient secretary had pruned the applicants to a short list.

'Well?' he said quite gently, but she knew she had better say something quickly, or he would put her down as mentally incompetent and have no compunction in throwing her out.

She launched into the little speech she had prepared, but he stopped her after a few minutes with a peremptory gesture and said, 'Most of that is in your application. Why do you want to work for me?'

There it was again—not, *why do you want to work for this firm,* but, *why do you want to work for me?*

'I don't,' she said, and was immediately aware that it was the wrong answer, but rashly didn't care. 'I need a job,' she said, 'and I liked the look of this one. I think I'd enjoy it, and I think I'd do it well.'

'Do you?' He glanced down at the papers before him on the desk, and she saw that neatly laid side by side in front of him were her letter of application, handwritten as requested in the advertisement, and the form she had filled out at his secretary's request. If he had glanced at that, he knew not only her full name, but that she was eighteen, that she was single, that she had left school with her University Entrance Examination accredited, a testament to her teachers' assessment of her intelligence and industry, that she had attended a secretarial course and passed with flying colours, had held a number of holiday jobs in the past couple of years, and could list several people who would be willing to give her a character reference.

The advertisement had said, 'Typist and relieving receptionist,' and she had liked the sound of the dual role, promising an occasional change from sitting all day in a typing pool.

'It sounds within my capabilities,' she said firmly.

'Maybe you should set your sights higher,' he suggested, but she had the feeling, in spite of the lack of emotion in his voice, that he was testing her.

'Perhaps I will, later,' she said. 'At the moment I've just left the secretarial college, and jobs are hard to find for people without experience, even if they have quite good qualifications.'

'So you'd leave us if something better came along?'

'Aren't there opportunities for advancement in the firm?' she asked.

He paused a moment and said, 'Yes, there are, for people with intelligence and initiative.'

She let her silence speak for itself, and she thought the shadow of a smile crossed his face, but it was gone in an instant.

'Are you interested in accountancy?' he asked her.

'Not especially, though I've had some basic courses in it. I prefer the secretarial side of business.'

'Well, you won't have your sights set on *my* job, then,' he murmured, and she stared a little because that sounded like a joke, though his face remained impassive.

'I'm sure your typing is up to standard,' he said, looking again at the pages in front of him. 'You take shorthand as well?' As she nodded he said, 'It isn't a requirement, but it might be useful sometimes. You'd be on the reception desk for a couple of hours most afternoons. Our receptionist finishes the day at three; she has a young family. Do you like working with the public?'

'I'm sure I will.'

'It's an important job, the front line of the business, first impression and all that,' he said. 'Do you ever smile, Miss Lovegrove?'

'I'm nervous,' she said. She supposed she should turn on a smile to demonstrate her ability in that direction, but she refused to grin like a Cheshire cat for this cold, superior being.

'Really,' he said, with a dry inflection. 'It isn't apparent.'

She didn't answer that, and after a moment he said, 'You know the terms and conditions?'

'Yes.' They had been set out very clearly in the letter which had requested her presence for an interview.

'Do you have any questions?'

'Do I get the job?' she demanded.

'We'll let you know,' he assured her smoothly, and stood up. She supposed that was a clear indication that the interview was over, and she murmured a polite thanks and made for the door. She had a nasty feeling that he had decided she wouldn't do. She had said too much, or not enough, or the wrong thing. In the doorway she turned, her brown eyes unconsciously appealing, trying to assess what sort of impression she had made on him. He was watching her calmly, still on his feet as he waited politely for her to leave. She couldn't read any expression in the chilly blue eyes. Suddenly, without any premeditation at all, she blurted, 'At least I'm not blond!'

He didn't look annoyed, or amused, or even surprised. He stood just exactly as he was, and his expression remained exactly the same. 'No, you're not blond,' he agreed gravely.

Outside, a gust of wind caught her as the glass outer door closed with silent, automatic efficiency behind her. The day had been balmily sunny when she had entered the building, but Wellington was notorious for its winds, which were both capricious and forceful. The capital, with its buildings hugging the edges of the harbour that opened onto Cook Strait at the southernmost tip of the North Island and climbing back into the hills that surrounded the waterfront, could be the most charmingly interesting of New Zealand's cities. But when the wind was in a vicious mood, life was a grim struggle against the elements, the inhabitants pitting their wits against gales which could blow a man off his feet or send a housewife's carefully pegged washing sailing from the suburban hills over the city to the sea, irretrievably lost.

To Larissa, the sudden change seemed an omen. She had entered the offices of T. J. Sharpe with high hopes and with a modicum of confidence that she could make a good impression and secure her future. But Mr. Sharpe had been less than impressed, and his manner, like the wind that now chilled her skin and sent a shiver through her body, had been cold and unfriendly. And she supposed he must have thought her final remark impertinent. Well, she shrugged, trying to be philosophical, there were other jobs. This was only the third she had applied for. She had told herself this morning, third time lucky, but . . .

So it was with pleased surprise that she learned the following day that she had been accepted, after all. The secretary phoned her and told her to present herself the following Monday morning.

'Thank you!' she stammered. 'Thank you very much!'

A little repressively, the woman said, 'Don't thank me, Miss Lovegrove. Mr. Sharpe made the decision.'

Larissa wondered if the slightly disapproving tone meant that if he had taken his secretary's advice she would not have got the job. But she didn't suppose that the advice had been asked for. Her guess was that Mr. Sharpe definitely made his own decisions.

The first day, she didn't see him at all. And, concentrating on the task of assimilating her duties and discovering what was expected of her, she had little time to think about him. The next day, however, when she had taken over the reception desk from the pleasant young married woman who presided over it for most of the day, he left the building early, and as he made to pass the desk, she said, 'Good afternoon, Mr. Sharpe.'

He stopped and said, 'Good afternoon, Miss Lovegrove. Is everything going smoothly?'

She wondered if he was concerned for her personally, or for his business, since she was such a new and untried representative of the firm. But she said, 'Yes, thank you. Mr. Sharpe—I want to thank you for giving me the job.'

He didn't make any reply to that, but he didn't move away, either. A little flustered by the cool scrutiny he was giving her, she said, 'I'm sorry if I was a bit—cheeky, the other day. I didn't mean to be.'

'If I'd thought you did, you wouldn't have got the job,' he said coldly. Then he added, 'You weren't meant to hear, of course, but if I offended you, I apologise.'

His clipped tones didn't sound in the least apologetic, only faintly bored, but he had used the word, and she nearly fell off her chair with astonishment.

'Th-that's all right,' she assured him. 'I expect I was feeling rather strung up and oversensitive.'

He raised his brows a little, and she wondered if it was beyond his comprehension that anyone should allow a little thing like applying for their first job to unstring them, but he didn't say anything further, just nodded to her and left.

She soon became accustomed to the work and came to know the other staff members. There were two other typists, both married, who shared the room where she spent the majority of the day, and who made her welcome and helped her in the first few weeks until she found her feet. The other women on the staff were further up the office social scale, one a senior accountant and the other Mr. Sharpe's secretary, Miss Collins. There were several young men who were lordly about giving orders in the typing pool, and had an office each, and who tried not to show their slight awe of the boss. One of them, Gareth Selby, began to make a habit of lingering by the reception desk when Larissa was on duty, teasing her with compliments until she blushed, and laughing at her innocence and embarrassment over his half-understood innuendos.

She wasn't sure if she liked him, but he was good-looking in a slightly raffish way, quite unlike her imagined picture of a staid accountant, and she could not help but be a little flattered that this apparently worldly-wise, good-looking young man obviously found her attractive, if somewhat naïve.

The first time he asked her to join him for a drink after work, she turned him down, and as T. J. Sharpe walked in just as Gareth was leaning persuasively over her desk, his hand reaching for hers, he had no opportunity to make her change her mind. He straightened so suddenly he almost lost his balance, and to her annoyance, Larissa felt herself flushing as she glanced apprehensively at her employer's face. But he gave no sign that he had noticed anything, merely nodding to them both without speaking as he progressed towards his own office.

The next time, Gareth picked his moment better, and when she said baldly that she was too young to go into a hotel bar, he looked astonished and then amused. 'Good heavens, darling, surely you know it's done all the time!' he said.

'Not by me,' she said firmly.

'You could pass for twenty,' he told her, slipping bold eyes over her slim figure.

'It's against the law.'

He looked impatient, but then he laughed and suggested dinner instead, since she was such a law-abiding young woman, and within a few minutes she had let him persuade her. She enjoyed the evening and found him good company. Afterwards, he kissed her good-night, of course, outside the flat she shared with a girl friend. But when his lips became passionate and invasive, she stopped him, and he accepted the rebuff with a humorous air of resignation that emphasised her youth and inexperience, and made her feel something of a prude.

It wasn't her first kiss, but those she had received before had been given by clumsy boys, not sophisticated, handsome men, and she had definitely enjoyed it before she pushed him away, when caution got the better of sexual instinct. She was a little wary of this new experience, but for several days she responded to his knowing glances, his whispered remarks and occasional touches, as he passed her at her desk or in one of the narrow passageways, with a shy but pleased acceptance. She wondered when he would ask her out again, and remembered with pleasure the feel of firm male lips on hers, and with relief, the fact that he had let her stop him quite easily. She wouldn't let matters go too far too fast, and Gareth, she thought, was not attempting to rush her. It didn't occur to her that he was too experienced to scare her by clumsy haste. She believed that their relationship held a warm promise, and she smiled at him happily when he stopped by her desk and didn't pull back when his fingers flicked her cheek or touched her hair in passing. He was deliberately making her aware of him, so that even the occasional chill stare they evoked from T. J. Sharpe as he came on them laughing together or found Gareth sitting casually on the edge of her desk, her smiling face lifted to his teasing one, scarcely impinged on her consciousness.

The bubble burst when one of the other typists casually mentioned Gareth's wife. Larissa never knew if the casualness was feigned to spare her feelings, but it jolted her out of her rosy dream world and abruptly changed her manner towards Gareth.

He was puzzled, of course, and persistent, too, and when she finally said flatly, 'I didn't know you were married,' he laughed and pretended disbelief. She looked at him then with contempt and said, 'You knew very well I wouldn't have gone out with you and let you kiss me if I had known.'

'You never asked.' He shrugged. 'It's no secret. Don't you girls in the typing room gossip among yourselves?'

'We have better things to do than talk about creeps like you!'

'Thanks, darling. You've got a temper under that sweet little madonna-face, haven't you?' He tipped his head to one side, looking at her consideringly, but with a malicious light in his eyes. 'Temper goes with a passionate nature. You could be a hot little number if you tried, you know—you kiss very nicely when you let yourself go a bit.'

The cutting reply on her lips died as she realised that the door had opened and was swinging gently behind Mr. Sharpe as his cool blue eyes rested for a moment on her flushed face and then passed impassively to the still-smiling Gareth.

Gareth shoved a hand casually into one of his pockets, nodded pleasantly to his boss and moved away without haste. The other man was still standing just inside the doorway, and his expression was even more glacial than usual. Then he, too, moved and he strode past her without even acknowledging the rather shaken greeting she gave him.

In the following months she gained confidence in her work and learned more about the business side of T. J. Sharpe. No one seemed to know much about his private life, though occasionally a beautifully groomed, glamorous blond woman appeared, sweeping confidently into his office with a casual word to Miss Collins; later she was superseded by an equally glamorous redhead. But about his business career there was no secret. He had been employed by a big firm of accountants, had early branched out on his own and built up a creditable clientele, then had moved into the financial advice and investment field, and was regarded as a very up-and-coming young man, on his way to becoming one of New Zealand's few millionaires. In the tricky arena of finance and investment, he had never been known to put a foot wrong. A sharp brain, a cool head, and an intuitive flair for making money made him both respected and in some ways feared in the financial world.

When she first heard one of the senior executives call him Tristan, she had to suppress a breath of laughter. One of the other typists glanced at her curiously, and she whispered, 'Good heavens! Do people really give their children names like that?'

The girl looked blank, and slightly shocked, and Larissa decided not to explain. It probably wouldn't seem funny to anyone else, anyway. The two men were standing yards away, and he couldn't possibly have heard, and yet as he turned he shot her a blue glance that seemed rapier sharp. She actually quivered for a moment, the laughter dying abruptly from her eyes. He really was a very disquieting man.

When Miss Collins became ill suddenly and was rushed off to hospital for an emergency operation, Larissa was surprised to be called into Tristan Sharpe's office and told she was to become his temporary secretary.

'But why me?' she asked blankly.

He raised his brows slightly and gave her a look that conveyed icy displeasure. Evidently he didn't approve any questioning of his decisions. After a moment, however, he did deign to answer her. 'Why not you?' he asked.

'Well, because I'm the most junior typist,' she said, 'and I have the least experience—'

'But the best and most recent qualifications,' he said. 'The other girls are rusty in their shorthand, and they're not ambitious, not career women. If Miss Collins was not coming back, of course I would find a more experienced secretary to take her place. As it is, the job is temporary, two months at most while she recovers, and I think if you're willing to extend yourself and I'm patient, you could probably cope for that time. It will be more convenient for me and useful experience for you.'

'*Will* you be patient?'

'Don't you think I'm capable of it?' he asked dryly.

If you want something badly enough, she thought. Aloud, she said, 'You don't seem the kind of person to suffer fools gladly.'

'Are you a fool?'

'No.' She lifted her head and met the cold eyes with a sparkling challenge in her own.

'Then the question doesn't arise, does it? I have some letters that need to be sent right away. You should be able to find what you need in Miss Collins's desk.'

It was exhilarating, working so closely with him, she found, though slightly nerve-racking. He tolerated no lapses due to carelessness or inattention, though he kept his promise to be patient when she had to ask for his instructions on things that Miss Collins would no doubt have known without asking. She began to learn to read the slight movements of his firm mouth and the rare glint of humour or annoyance that appeared in his eyes. It became a challenge to her to be able to gauge his moods in spite of the rigid control that he kept over himself. She was able to recognise the still, narrow-eyed look he assumed when he was presented with a problem requiring a swift decision, the way he occasionally massaged the back of his neck with his hand when he had been under tension, the way he lowered his eyelids and leaned back in his chair when he was bored, and the fact that when he was angry he never raised his voice, but a steel thread ran through the biting remarks with which he could wither an erring staff member or an opponent.

Sometimes she would look a warning when one of the young men breezed through the outer office on his way to see Tristan, and gradually they came to rely on her discreet signals, proceeding with caution if she shook her head, and giving a relieved grin back to her if she smiled and gave a small thumbs-up sign. It was a game, and she enjoyed the sense of camaraderie that emanated from it. It made life more pleasant all round.

One day, when she had given the thumbs-up signal, the young man didn't realise that the adjoining door was open as he said cheerfully, 'In a good mood, is he? Thanks, sweetie!'

Larissa gave him an anguished look and indicated the door, and his grin faded as he grimaced an apology, shrugged, and went in with the air of a Daniel about to make an acquaintance with a lion or two.

She heard the grim note with which Tristan ordered him to shut the door, and she briefly raised her eyes in a despairing little prayer before she returned her attention quite fiercely to the task of transcribing a letter Tristan had dictated that morning.

When the young man emerged, Tristan was right behind him, and after he had left, she felt the implacable presence at her side and knew she had to face it.

She looked up with a bright half smile and said, 'Did you want something, Mr. Sharpe?'

'So you think you can read my moods?' he enquired silkily.

A little breathlessly, she said, 'Sometimes.'

'You're too modest. It seems the whole office relies on your interpretation of my feelings.'

'That's nonsense!' she said, trying to sound brisk. 'Any good secretary tries to understand her employer's moods. It's part of the job.'

'Good lord! Is that what they taught you at that college?'

'Yes, one of the things. I'm sure Miss Collins tried to do the same.'

'If she did, I've never noticed it. And I'm quite sure Miss Collins didn't share her knowledge with my entire staff. Didn't they teach you anything about discretion at that place?'

'Yes, of course.' Her voice was wooden, her eyes on the typewriter in front of her. 'I haven't given away any secrets. Just tried to oil the wheels a little.'

'You see that as part of your job, too, no doubt.'

She heard the sarcasm in his voice, and ignored it. 'Yes,' she said stubbornly.

'You'd do better to say you're sorry, and hope for the matter to be overlooked,' he warned.

She paused a moment, and then said, 'I don't think I am sorry.'

She was still staring hard at the keys of the typewriter, and for long seconds the only sound in the room was the hum of its electric motor. Then he said softly, 'Look at me, Miss Lovegrove.'

She looked reluctantly. He had leaned one hand on the desk and was bending over her slightly, but it still hurt her neck a little to turn and face him.

'Don't you realise that I could make you sorry?' he asked, with soft menace. 'Very sorry, in fact.'

'Sack me, you mean?' She swallowed nervously, but didn't look away. 'Do you think an apology obtained under duress is any good?'

'Meaning you won't apologise?'

'I will if you insist but I don't see the necessity for it.'

'Thereby robbing it of any meaning.'

'That depends on what you expect to gain, doesn't it?'

He shifted, so that he was sitting on the desk, looking down at her, and folded his arms. He looked grim, but the steel had left his voice as he said, 'I think you had better explain that.'

'If you wanted me to—to see the error of my ways, you haven't succeeded. But if you just mean to demonstrate how you can force people to do what you say, and you don't care if it's only out of fear—then you'll have got what you wanted.'

'You see me as a bully,' he said.

'No, I don't. I think you're a very determined man, and you usually get what you want because you don't pull any punches when you go after it.'

'Go on,' he encouraged, and she smiled faintly, because in spite of himself he was intrigued, and she knew that was the egoist in him. 'Why are you smiling?' he demanded.

'You can't possibly want to know what an eighteen-year-old typist thinks of you.'

'I'm beginning to think you're a most unusual eighteen-year-old typist, and anyway, at the moment you're my secretary. Tell me what my mood is now.'

She looked at him carefully and said slowly, 'You're annoyed, but not as angry as you were a few minutes ago. And—surprised, I think. And just a little bit amused, rather unwillingly amused. Why do you try to repress your sense of humour?'

'Count yourself lucky that I have it, young woman,' he said, getting off the desk and straightening up. 'And no more smoke signals, please. My moods and feelings are my private business, and no one else's.'

For a few minutes after he had returned to his own office, she sat there doing nothing, feeling as though the edge of a storm had brushed her and mercifully passed on.

There was a locked storage room where certain confidential files and papers were kept. Larissa had been hunting for some time one day for a file Tristan Sharpe had asked for, when she was interrupted by Gareth Selby.

'Looking for something?' he asked pleasantly.

She explained, distractedly running her hand along a shelf, counting off the alphabetical labels on the bulky files. 'It *should* be here,' she said. 'Unless it's filed under something else, and I can't think what.'

He found it for her, and she put out her hand, smiling gratefully at him. 'Oh, thank you, Gareth!' Tristan was in a taut, chilly mood, and she didn't want to have to return and tell him she couldn't find the file.

But Gareth didn't give it to her; he held it up out of her reach and said, 'Well, thank me properly then, little Miss Prude.'

'Gareth, please don't be silly! He's waiting for it.'

She made the mistake of trying to grab it and he moved quickly so that she cannoned up against him. His arms went around her swiftly, the file falling with a thud on the floor, and his lips came down on hers.

She pushed at his upper arms and tried to move her head back away from him, but his mouth stayed firmly on hers and he pulled her closer, his hands roving over her body. Larissa shuddered, doubled her hands into fists, and beat at his arms and shoulders, but it seemed nothing was going to stop him. He tried to part her lips with his tongue, but she was outraged and revolted by his behaviour, and whatever response he had won from her before, there was none for him now.

It was stuffy and airless in the small room, and

Gareth had pushed the door almost closed behind them. His embrace, his kiss, were suffocating, and for a few moments she thought she might faint. Her struggles became less determined as she tried to draw breath.

Gareth gave a little grunt of satisfaction, and his hands became bolder. She shuddered and tried again to release herself, and then an icy voice said, 'I suggest you two confine your lovemaking to outside office hours, if you don't mind.'

Gareth let her go so quickly she staggered against one of the shelves, and she was still clutching it for support after he had brushed, red-faced, past Tristan Sharpe and left her white and shaking with reaction, her eyes bright with shock and fear as they rested on Tristan's coldly furious face.

'We weren't . . .' she stammered. 'I wasn't . . . I didn't invite that! Oh, I'm so glad you came!'

Her lips were trembling terribly, and her eyes stung with tears, and his cold face changed a little, a frown line forming between his brows. He instinctively reached out a hand to her as she came shakily away from the shelf and swayed, biting her lip and trying to blink the tears away.

She felt the grip of his fingers on her arm, and then his other arm went round her and she let her head fall against his chest, and sobbed for a few minutes. And, astonishingly, he let her do it, his hand moving with a soothing motion on her back.

She realised with sudden appalled shock what she was doing, and broke away from him, gabbling, 'I'm sorry, I didn't mean to—I'm sorry to be such a nuisance. I'm all right now.'

'You little fool,' he said unemotionally. 'What the devil did you think you were asking for all this time, if not—*that!*—as you so bluntly put it?'

Dismayed, she said, 'What do you mean—all this time? I haven't—'

'You have,' he interrupted in a hard voice. 'You'd scarcely been here a week before you were letting him touch you at every opportunity and whisper sweet nothings in your ear. You've kissed him, before—I've heard you discussing it. Didn't your mother warn you about leading a man on? If you weren't willing to come through, you shouldn't have encouraged him to think you would.'

Stung, she said, 'I haven't *got* a mother! And I didn't encourage him at all—at least, not since I found out he was married! I've scarcely spoken to him since then, and if you're so observant, I'm surprised you didn't notice *that!*'

'You haven't had much chance since you began acting as my secretary. It took you out of his way.'

'I was keeping out of his way before that! I didn't *want* him to kiss me. He just grabbed me, and I couldn't—he's much too strong!'

His eyes narrowed, and she knew he was thinking, weighing her story against what he had seen, in the past and just now. 'Is that the truth?' he said tersely.

'Yes, it is,' she said huskily. 'I swear it!'

His eyes went hard and flinty. Softly, he said, 'I'll show him the door!'

Larissa gaped. 'Sack him? But you can't . . . his wife . . . !'

He looked at her coldly. 'You don't want to be rid of him?'

'Not if it means he loses his job! He might have children. . . .'

'He does!'

'Then you mustn't—please! You can't punish a whole family for what he did. It will probably never happen again.'

'I promise you it won't,' he said flatly. Then, 'If he ever lays so much as a finger on you again, you're to tell me, understand?'

'Yes,' she said uncertainly. 'Yes. Thank you.'

'Is that the file I wanted, that you're standing on?' he asked, and she moved hastily and said, 'Yes. Yes, it is.' She picked it up and he waved for her to precede him out of the stuffy little room and down the passageway. When they reached his office she placed the file on his desk, and he said, 'Thank you,' as though nothing had happened, as though she had just returned from her search and he had never left his office. He sat down and began to leaf through the typed pages. 'It's all right,' he said. 'You can go back to your typewriter.' Then, as she reached the door, he said, 'Larissa . . .'

He had never called her by her first name before, and now he said it as though there was something slightly funny about it, but she was too grateful to be angry. She turned and looked back at him, and he said, 'Smile. It isn't the end of the world.'

She managed a trembly curve of her lips, but said, '*You* never smile.'

'I don't have much to smile about,' he said, sounding jaded. 'You're young and the world's at your feet—or could be. Go on, there's a good girl.'

She went, with a lift of her heart. She wondered what he would be like if he did smile. Quite different, she imagined. She was sure he could be tender and loving when he dropped the icy mask. The next time the svelte redhead came in and passed by her with a smile and a quick word, she found herself clenching her hands in her lap and wondering, with a peculiar ache in the pit of her stomach, whether Tristan dropped the mask for *her.*

When the girl had left, and Larissa took some letters in for his signature, she found herself studying him minutely for any change in his manner, or any sign that he had been less than his usual coldly contained self.

He looked up and said, 'Something on your mind?'

Larissa shook her head. His shirt was quite uncrumpled, his hair as sleek and his tie as securely knotted as ever, and his blue eyes had acquired no added warmth. If the redheaded girl friend stirred his emotions at all, he was very good at hiding the results.

Chapter Three

Some crisis blew up. There was a day of tension, telephone calls, hurried conferences; and Larissa for the first time saw Tristan react to stress by snapping at her when she didn't produce a file quite quickly enough. She said nothing, merely smiled a little when she handed over the file, and he flicked her a cold glance and took it, his mouth compressed in a hard line.

After it was all over, every loose end apparently satisfactorily tied up, they had both worked into the night, and not eaten anything but the biscuits Larissa had served with cups of coffee, since lunch.

'I'll give you a meal and take you home,' Tristan said, dropping some papers into a drawer of his desk and standing up, so that Larissa came out of her chair, too.

'It isn't necessary,' she said.

'Don't argue, there's a good girl,' he said shortly, but she was surprised to detect a hint of weariness in his voice.

'You don't need to, if you'd rather go home to bed.'

'I would not rather go home,' he said. 'Do I look as though I need my bed?'

'No.'

He looked just as he always did, aloof and unemotional and arrogantly sure of himself.

'Then shut up and do as you're told, will you?'

She collected her bag and jacket and, feeling rather cross, followed him out of the building and waited while he unlocked his low, shiny car and let her in. His mouth was thin as he joined her, and they didn't speak until he ushered her into a deeply carpeted, expensive-looking restaurant, and they were shown to a table.

'Do you like seafood?' he asked her.

'Yes.'

'They do a particularly good seafood salad here. Like to try it?'

'All right.'

'Such enthusiasm,' he murmured sarcastically. He returned his attention to the menu, and when the waiter came ordered fruit appetisers for them both, and the salads, and then a bottle of sauterne to go with it.

When the waiter filled her glass, she looked a little apprehensively at it, and Tristan Sharpe said, 'It won't hurt you, and I have no intention of making you drunk. I don't seduce eighteen-year-old typists, either drunk or sober, if that's what's bothering you.'

She supposed that fatigue and hunger were making him more than usually disagreeable tonight but she was tired and hungry too. 'I'm nineteen, actually,' she said sharply. 'And I'm your secretary, at the moment.'

His hand, which had been slowly revolving his wineglass, stilled, and there was a noticeable pause before he said, 'Well, so you've had a birthday. Congratulations.'

'Thank you.' Her throat hurt for some reason, and her voice was husky as she said, staring at the immaculate tablecloth, 'I'm not used to drinking.'

He gave an exasperated little laugh, and she looked up, startled, because she had never heard him laugh before. 'Good heavens, child!' he said. 'Having a glass of wine with a meal isn't *drinking!* Where on earth were you brought up?'

'In foster homes, mostly,' she answered tightly. 'Where were *you?*'

She raised her head to look challengingly at him, and for a moment he just looked back, a slight frown of annoyance between his brows, and his eyes decidedly frosty. Apparently she wasn't supposed to ask personal questions of *him.*

But then, surprisingly, he seemed to relax a trifle. 'Not with a silver spoon,' he said. 'But I had a mother and father, anyway.' He stopped there rather abruptly, and the curl of his mouth was unpleasant. Then he said, 'What happened to your parents?'

'My mother died when I was four. My father couldn't cope with . . . well . . . anything. He got housekeepers at first, but none of them lasted long. He began drinking heavily, and when he lost his job the social welfare took me over and found a foster home. They try to place children permanently but it doesn't always work out.'

'How many foster homes did you have?'

'Three. It's not so bad. Some children have many more.'

'Where's your father now?'

'We lost touch years ago, but they told me he had died when I was sixteen.'

'No brothers or sisters?'

'No.' There had been temporary 'families,' and some she had been fond of, had felt wrenchingly the parting from them when it came. She still remembered Susan, who had been her little 'sister' until

Susan's father got a job in Australia and the family had gone, leaving her for Social Welfare to place again in another home; and Jeffrey, who had shared the same foster home for five years before his mother reclaimed him at the age of fourteen. She and Jeffrey had been close, and promised to keep in touch, but his mother had not encouraged the contact, and she supposed Jeffrey, having found a real family, didn't need a pretend sister any more. After six months the exchange of letters had stopped, and she had not seen him since.

'Who paid for your training?' Tristan asked.

'The state. With the help of what I earned in the holiday jobs I took.'

'And now you're on your own.'

'More or less. I share a flat with a girl I met at the college. She's a good friend.'

Their meal was served, and he saw her reach for her wineglass and said, 'You don't have to drink that if you don't like it.'

She sipped it and said, 'I think I do like it. And the salad is fantastic.'

'Good.' He sounded bored, and she dipped her head and concentrated on the food on her plate.

He didn't ask if she wanted dessert, but ordered a chocolate and ice cream confection for her, while he helped himself from a cheese board.

'I didn't ask for this,' she protested weakly.

'I feel like giving you a treat,' he said. 'You like chocolate and cream, don't you?'

She did, but she didn't see how he could have known it. 'Yes,' she admitted reluctantly. 'But I've already eaten so much. . . .'

He shrugged. 'I'm not forcing you.'

He was looking down, placing a piece of blue-vein cheese with precision on his cracker. It was absurd to imagine he would be disappointed if she didn't appreciate his 'treat.'

She picked up the spoon and tried it. It was light and delicious, and before she put down the spoon again, she had finished three quarters of it.

She pushed the crystal dish away and said, 'That was lovely. Thank you.'

'Coffee?'

'Yes, please.'

He signalled the waiter and then unexpectedly leaned forward a little, amusement in his eyes as he touched her upper lip with his finger. It came away with a smudge of chocolate and cream on it, and she thought he would wipe it off on his table napkin. Instead he lifted the finger to his own mouth. 'Mmm. Very nice,' he murmured. 'Don't look so startled, Larissa. I'm not about to eat *you!*'

Her mouth still tingled from that light, fleeting touch, and her heart was beating unevenly. He was watching her with slightly narrowed eyes, and she knew he was assessing her reaction, taking note of the slight flush of colour in her cheeks.

'I didn't think you were,' she said, somewhat foolishly. She looked away from him, and was glad to see the waiter come with their coffee.

She concentrated on stirring sugar into hers, avoiding the sardonic blue gaze that she knew was bent on her.

Almost under his breath, he said suddenly, 'You are *young*, aren't you?'

She raised her eyes, because he sounded sardonically impatient, and he said, 'If you think I'm going to pounce on you on the way home, you can stop worrying. I'm not Gareth Selby!'

'I wasn't thinking anything of the kind!'

'I can read you like a book!' he said contemptuously. 'And most of the pages are still blank.'

'You can't! You thought I was encouraging Gareth, knowing he was married.'

'Ages ago!' he said, moving his hand with an impatient gesture.

'Why didn't you say something?' she asked him. 'Would you have let it go on?'

'I don't interfere in the private lives of my staff. That went out with the Victorians.'

'But if you thought I was such a child. . . .'

'Most girls of eighteen these days seem to know their way about. I didn't realise you were any exception—then.'

'What makes you think I am?'

'What do you think? The day you wept all over me in the storage room, of course. Only an innocent could have got so worked up about a mere kiss, however unwelcome.'

'I see. You think I'm a fool, don't you?'

'You said yourself I don't suffer fools gladly. Shall I tell you something? I'll be quite sorry to see Miss Collins come back.'

Something like shock ran through her. Her first thought was that he was being kind, but that sort of kindness didn't seem part of his nature. She glanced up at him, and the curve of his mouth held cynicism, and his eyes self-mockery.

'Thank you,' she said. 'I'll be sorry, too.'

'How sweet. Shall we go before we get maudlin about it?' He stood up and pulled out her chair, and they didn't speak again until they were in the car, and he had driven out of the parking space into the traffic.

Quietly seething, she said, 'Why do you have to be so beastly?'

'Am I?' he said, and shrugged. 'Forgive me. I'm not used to dealing with the young and innocent.'

'Oh, do stop harping on my youth!' she snapped. 'You're not Methuselah, are you?'

Into the little silence that followed, she said quickly, 'I'm sorry.'

'I'm sure you are,' he said calmly. 'Is it a right turn here?'

'Yes.' She kept her lips firmly closed, then, except when he asked for directions, until they drew up outside the flat.

'Thank you very much,' she said. 'For the meal and for bringing me home.'

'Have a good sleep,' he said. 'I won't roar if you're late in tomorrow.'

'You never roar.'

'Is that a point in my favour?'

'I don't know,' she answered truthfully. 'A restrained snarl is sometimes more frightening than a full-throated roar.'

'So I snarl, do I?'

'Occasionally—in a terribly civilised way.'

Amused, he said, 'You make me sound like a domesticated tiger.'

In a strange way, the description fitted, and she couldn't suppress a small gurgle of laughter. She saw a quick movement of his head and said, 'I'm sorry, but you lead me on to say these things. It's unfair, if you don't want to hear them!'

'Perhaps I do,' he said, somewhat ambiguously. 'Go on, now. I'll see you tomorrow.'

The casual words sounded oddly like a promise. She slipped out of the car with a swift, 'Good night,' and ran up the small flight of steps that led to the flat. In the doorway she switched on the light, and turned to wave, but it was too dark to see if he had waved back before the car moved off down the hill.

Miss Collins came back, and Larissa returned to the typing room and reception desk with very real regret. It had not always been comfortable working closely with Tristan Sharpe, but she had enjoyed the stimulation of it. She missed the challenge, the need to be on her toes all the time, and the odd pleasure of now and then pitting herself against his astringent comments.

She watched him a little wistfully one day as he crossed the reception area towards his office, nodding her a wordless greeting, and then he turned and stopped dead, catching her expression.

Larissa bent her head over the typewriter in front of her and struck a succession of keys at random. The result was gibberish, of course, and she tore the paper crossly out of the machine and screwed it into a ball, flinging it into the wastebasket beside her.

Tristan was standing by the desk when she looked up. 'Something the matter, Miss Lovegrove?' he asked.

'Anyone can make a mistake, Mr. Sharpe,' she said tartly.

'You don't seem to be enjoying your work.'

Suddenly irritated by the light mockery in his voice, she said, 'I'm thinking of leaving.'

There was no change of expression on his face, yet she had the feeling she had given him a slight and unpleasant shock. 'The hell you are,' he said, quite lightly, making her eyes widen at his language, although his voice was very quiet. 'Don't I pay you enough?'

'Money isn't everything,' she told him succinctly.

'So why do you want to leave?'

She could hardly say she hadn't thought of it until just this minute. 'This isn't as interesting as—as working as your temporary secretary,' she admitted almost angrily.

A slight smile touched his hard mouth, and softly he said, 'Do you miss me, Larissa?'

She simply stared back at him, blindingly aware that it was true. She missed his infuriating, calculating, mocking manner, the quickness of his mind, the subtle pleasure of watching him make each faultless move in the complicated financial manoeuvres he specialised in, and of recognising the fleeting gleam of satisfaction or the reluctant glint of humour in his eyes when he allowed the mask to slip momentarily from his icily controlled face.

He watched her, waiting for an answer, and when it didn't come, he said, 'Have dinner with me tonight.'

'Why?' she asked blankly.

One corner of his mouth quirked a little, and his brows rose a fraction. With marked coolness, as though she was a singularly stupid young woman, he said, 'Because you're pretty and I've missed you, of course. I'll pick you up at seven . . . unless you're busy tonight?'

His frosty glance dared her to say that she was, and she just faintly shook her head, bemused by the invitation. After he had gone she still couldn't believe it, going over his words in her mind. He had said—he *had* said—that she was pretty, that he missed her . . . but he had sounded impatient about it, almost resentful.

She dressed with great care that night, her nerves jumpy, still incredulous and almost expecting him not to turn up. In fact, he was very punctual. She met him at the door, her eyes still faintly disbelieving as she took in the dark suit and the pleated evening shirt he wore. He flicked a look over her swirling brown velvet skirt and champagne-coloured ruffled silk blouse, and forbore to comment. Anxious, she said, 'I didn't know where you were taking me. Is this all right?'

'Of course it's all right,' he said. 'You look very lovely.'

She thanked him doubtfully; he didn't sound at all overwhelmed, only very slightly bored, and after he had seated her and started the car he drove without speaking, his profile remote and unfeeling when she glanced at it.

He still seemed remote as they sat opposite each other at a small table overlooking the dark curve of the harbour, its contour outlined by a crescent of city lights. Superimposed on the night view was a reflection of the tables behind them, the smartly dressed clientele of the restaurant all apparently engrossed in conversation between mouthfuls. But the man opposite her was silent, leaning slightly back in his chair as they waited for their order to arrive. Larissa was tense and unhappy, wishing he would say something, trying desperately to think of some acceptable small talk to fill in the silence between them.

She glanced up and found his hard gaze resting on her. Her eyes fell to the table, and she nervously touched the cutlery before her, making finger smudges on the polished silver.

'Stop fidgeting,' Tristan said. 'What's the matter?'

Her eyes flew up again, and then down. 'Nothing,' she muttered. Then she said quickly, 'I'm sorry, I don't know how to talk to you.'

'What on earth do you mean? You've done all right up until now.'

'I mean—' she glanced about the room—'everyone else seems to be having a good time.'

'And you're not? Then *I* should be apologising, not you. What would you like? Shall I make you laugh?' His glance flicked to a nearby party of four who were evidently sharing a hilarious joke. 'Or shall I hold your hand and nuzzle your ear like our friend in the corner there?' She followed his look as he gave a sardonic nod in the direction of a young couple who sat close together, whispering and starry-eyed.

Her face warmed, and she stared woodenly at the table and said in a low voice, 'I wasn't complaining, and I think you know it. I don't know why you asked me out, but I know I'm boring you, and—'

Her hand was suddenly covered in a hard clasp.

'You are not boring me,' he said distinctly. 'I thought I'd made it clear that I'd asked you out because I like your company, and your looks.' He paused. 'Don't you realise that I enjoy looking at you?'

Startled brown eyes met his. His eyes had narrowed slightly, and they looked very blue. Larissa swallowed before she said huskily, 'I'm—flattered. But—I don't understand.'

'Do you rate your own attractions so low?'

'I've never thought they could match *your* standards.'

'What would you know about my . . . standards?'

'I've seen your girl friends.'

'At the moment I don't have one.'

She moved her hand, but his grip remained firm, and his cool stare stayed rather mercilessly on her flushed, wary face. 'Are you—are you offering me the vacant position?' she asked him.

Smoothly, he said, 'Are you interested?'

A faint shiver of apprehension and excitement made her fingers quiver in his. 'I don't think I would interest *you* for long,' she said frankly, recalling the redhead and her predecessor.

'It's a bad habit to underestimate yourself,' he said, sounding rather curt. He released her hand suddenly and leaned back again, thrusting his own hand carelessly into a trouser pocket.

Larissa said, '*You* said I was like a book with blank pages.'

'Maybe I'd like to help you fill them. You haven't answered my question.'

Was she interested? It hadn't seriously occurred to her to think of him in that way. But the prospect of getting close to this enigmatic, infuriating man was intriguing. Caution warned her that it could also be dangerous. She *was* young, and more inexperienced than most girls of her age, and he was neither. She could end up being badly hurt. . . .

'Well?' he asked, his tone peremptory.

No! common sense told her. But she said slowly, 'That depends on what might be involved.'

'Oh, wise young virgin!' he mocked. 'I'm not asking you to go to bed with me—not yet, at any rate. You *are* a virgin, aren't you?'

'Yes.' She met his eyes stubbornly and said, 'I'm too young for you, aren't I?'

'Meaning that I'm too old for you.'

'You're not married, are you?'

'Surely the office grapevine must have relayed that information.'

'I never asked. But I gathered . . .'

'You gathered right. I've never been married.'

Their meal came, and she was glad of the interruption. It gave her a breathing space, and when Tristan spoke again, it was on a different subject altogether, as though he too preferred to leave the previous conversation in abeyance.

Of course he had ordered wine, and Larissa drank it rather recklessly, considering she was unused to it. Tristan watched her narrowly, refilling her glass without comment when she emptied it, keeping up a light, almost teasing conversation between courses, surprising her into a small laugh once or twice, but not holding her hand again.

There was a small dance floor and a three-piece orchestra through an archway, and as they waited for their coffee, Tristan surprised her by urging her to her feet and saying, 'Let's dance.'

'I never thought of you as a dancing man,' she murmured, as he pulled her closely into his arms, and she found her feet and body following him with rare perfection.

'I suspect you never thought of me as a man,' he replied, his voice notably dry.

His hand shifted from her waist and began moving lightly on her back, a deliberate caress. Larissa lifted her head and stared at him. She wasn't sure that he had meant what he had said before, or whether he had merely been indulging in a sophisticated brand of teasing. He was definitely trying to draw some response from her now, but his own face remained almost expressionless, his eyes holding no emotion except the dispassionate interest of a scientist conducting an experiment.

Anger stirred in her, and she said sharply, 'Stop it!'

She tried to pull away from him a little, putting some space between them. His hands slid to her waist, and he held her there, his thighs moving against hers in the rhythm of the dance. He watched her face, his eyebrows lifting slightly at the mutiny in her sparkling eyes. She was conscious of the most extraordinary sensations—a shocking desire to press herself closer to him, to let her own hands wander from their half-defensive position against his chest, to touch his shoulders and neck, and a shamed anger that he could deliberately arouse her like this while remaining unmoved himself.

The dance number came to an end, and although the band swung immediately into another, she pushed strongly away from Tristan and turned from him, going quickly back towards their table.

She drank her coffee in silence, not looking at him, and watched without meeting his eyes as he drank his at a more leisurely pace.

'Dance again, Larissa?' he asked, his tone holding mockery.

'No,' she said. 'No, thank you. Please take me home.'

She sat as far away from him in the car as her safety belt would allow, and he drove without speaking. Her hostile glance at his face told her nothing of his mood.

When he drew up outside her flat, she said stiltedly, 'Thank you, Mr. Sharpe. The dinner was delicious.'

She fumbled for the doorlatch, but her wrist was caught in a hard grasp, and he said, 'My name is Tristan. And we have things to talk about. Ask me in.'

She tentatively tried to move her hand from his, but his fingers retained their hold. Almost sulkily, she said, 'We'd disturb my flatmate.'

'Why are you angry?' he asked quietly.

'I don't like to be held by force.'

He let go her hand, and said, 'It isn't that. You were in a temper before we left the restaurant.'

'I am *not* in a temper!'

He laughed softly. 'Oh, yes you are. And I want to know why.'

'I thought you could read me like a book!' she reminded him scornfully.

'What about you?' he countered, and his hand went under her chin, turning her firmly to look up into his face. 'Tell me what mood I'm in now.'

The faint light from a street lamp showed little, only the grim line of his jaw and an odd glitter in his eyes, the rest of his face deeply shadowed.

'I don't know,' she said, her voice husky with sudden alarm. 'It's dark.'

'I'll give you a clue,' he said, and then his arm slid round her shoulders, pulling her close as he kissed her mouth.

His hand was on her throat, long fingers sensitively stroking the tautened line of it as her head went back against his arm. His mouth was surprisingly warm, firmly exploratory, making her lips part under his, kissing her deeply, with a slow, almost lazy hunger that made her heart pound with strange sensations as a wave of heat washed over her body.

Frightened by her own emotions, she raised a hand and clutched his sleeve, pulling ineffectually at it, and made a small, negative movement of her head.

Reluctantly, he lifted his mouth from hers, and she whispered agitatedly, 'Please—please don't!'

His fingers moved from her throat to her lips, gently touching them, and then softly brushed her cheek. Still holding her, he said, 'Why not?'

She didn't answer, trying to wriggle out of his arms, but he wouldn't permit it. "You didn't enjoy it?" he asked.

The detached curiosity in his voice ignited her anger again. She said furiously, 'Let me go!' Her nails dug into his wrist, trying to free herself.

'What a little spitfire you are!' His voice was amused, as he slackened his hold, but although he dropped his arms from her, he retained a grip on her wrist. 'I asked you a question.'

'I'd rather skip the postmortem,' she said, making an effort to emulate his self-control. 'I'm tired; let's call it a night, shall we?'

'You're not tired, you're scared,' he said, cynically. 'Maybe you *are* too young, at that.'

'You won't get me into bed by harping on my inexperience!'

Coldly, he said, 'It wasn't my intention. I'm a bit less crude than that, I hope! Actually, I was thinking aloud. You'd better forget what I said earlier.'

She didn't pretend not to know what he meant. 'I didn't think you were serious,' she said, striving for a light note, but it was difficult because she felt amazingly hurt, a spreading misery settling about her heart.

'You *are* young!' he said derisively.

'How old are *you?*' she asked him, her head back in challenge.

'I can give you a good ten years.'

'That's not so much!' she said, surprised.

'In terms of experience, it's a lifetime,' he said, his voice suddenly flat. 'Get inside, will you? I need a stiff drink, and I don't suppose you could offer one, even if you did ask me in.'

He leaned over and opened the door for her, and she got out, simmering at his brusque dismissal. Clearly, she said, 'Good night, Mr. Sharpe.'

She hoped that would annoy him, and perhaps it did, because he slammed the door without a reply, and the engine roared into life before she had reached her door.

Weeks went by when she scarcely saw him. He didn't come into the typing room, and if she was on the reception desk when he strode past he simply nodded without checking his pace, and her correct 'Good morning' or 'Good afternoon' floated after him as she watched him walk away.

Miss Collins stopped by her desk one day as she was typing accounts and placed a large manila envelope in front of her. 'Mr. Sharpe wants these, Larissa,' she said. 'Would you get a taxi and take them round, please.'

'I beg your pardon?' Larissa said, patently at sea.

'You don't know Mr. Sharpe is sick?' the woman asked, with a hint of impatience.

'No! Is it serious?'

'Of course not; he's to stay in bed for a few days, that's all. I can't leave the office while he's away, and he needs these. Some are simply to be signed—I've clipped them together with a note. And you'd better take a notebook, just in case. . . . Oh, here is the key. No need to get him out of bed to let you in.'

She gave Larissa the address and reminded her not to waste any time.

Larissa covered her typewriter and picked up the envelope and her bag, slipping a notebook and pencil into it before leaving. She felt reluctance, curiosity, and a vague anxiety as she sat stiffly in the taxi taking her along Lambton Quay and then out of the city centre to a road winding up into the surrounding hills. Eventually they drew up outside a modern town house built against a seemingly impossible slope, its bold architectural lines suggestive of determination and tenacity in the face of wind, weather, and the steep terrain to which it clung.

She used the key and stepped through a small entrance lobby into a room which was furnished with long black leather couches against a sand-coloured carpet and stark white walls leavened by two huge contemporary paintings in shades of blue and black. Decorator-designed, she decided, for Tristan Sharpe, and fitting his personality to a *T*.

His voice called sharply, 'Who is it?'

She saw the door at one side of the room half-ajar and went through into a bedroom. The carpet and walls were the same, the dressing table and built-in wardrobe dark satin-finished wood, and the coverlet that was slipping from the bed to the floor was hand-woven in deep golds and browns.

Tristan, wearing crumpled black judo-style pyjamas, was sitting against two badly stacked pillows, glaring at her. His face looked pale, and his eyes slightly bloodshot and glittery, and there was an unhealthy sheen of perspiration on his forehead.

'Why the devil did they send *you!*' he said irritably.

'I'm the junior,' she said. 'We get all the unpleasant jobs.'

The glitter in his eyes became angry and then changed to the faintest glint of amusement. 'Watch your tongue,' he advised dryly. 'I'm in the mood to play the heavy employer. You could find yourself without a job.'

She moved to pick up the slipping coverlet, and he snapped, 'Leave it! What have you got there?'

'Miss Collins said there are some letters to be signed, and some other papers you wanted.'

He took the envelope from her and slid out the contents, beginning to scan them. 'Sit down,' he said absently.

There was nowhere to sit but on the bed, and she remained standing. He glanced up, his mouth quirked a little, and then he returned his attention to the letters in his hand.

He groped, without looking up, on the table beside the bed, and she saw the silver ball-point pen there and picked it up, handing it to him.

Their fingers touched, and she drew back. He shot her a look and said, as he scribbled his signature on the letter in front of him, 'I'm not too sick to pick up a pen.'

'I'm so glad!' she said.

He looked up quickly. 'I told you to watch your tongue.'

'Yes, sir.'

His mouth tightened, and then he gave one of his oddly reluctant laughs. 'All right,' he said. 'I'm a brute, and I apologise. Being sick makes me bad-tempered.'

'Oh, is that what does it?' she asked ironically, and he said, 'I've apologised, but don't trade on it. Get yourself a chair, if it would compromise your virtue to sit on the bed. Can you take some notes and pass them on to Miss Collins?'

She did as he asked, sitting very correctly on a chair she had found in the dining alcove off the small kitchen. When at last he said, 'Right, that's all,' Larissa shut the notebook and replaced it in her bag, then looked up to find him lying back on the pillows with his eyes closed.

He opened them a moment later and shifted his shoulders, sitting more upright, but his mouth was tight and there was a drawn look about his eyes.

'Who's looking after you?' she asked.

'I don't need anyone,' he said. 'I can stagger as far as the bathroom and the kitchen. I'm not hungry, anyway, only thirsty.'

She glanced at the jug on the table beside him, and eyed the dusty-looking glass beside it. She went closer and peered into the jug. 'Fruit juice?' she asked.

He nodded, and she said, 'I'll get some fresh, if you have more.'

'In the kitchen. But it doesn't matter.' He frowned, and plucked at the front of his pyjama top, and she realised that it was damp with sweat. He looked paler, too, and as he picked up the papers she had brought she said, 'You shouldn't be working! Do you feel as bad as you look?'

'Flatterer!' he murmured, closing his eyes again. 'Probably.' He opened his eyes and glanced at her. 'Don't look so worried. It's a virus, something going round, according to the doctor. Go away, there's a good girl, before you get it, too.'

She didn't go away. She went to the kitchen and found the juice, then decided on impulse to make a cup of strong tea for him. She dropped ice cubes in the jug with the juice and, replacing it in the refrigerator, took the tea in to him.

'I thought you might prefer this,' she said. 'I'll bring the juice for later.'

He drained the tea, and she thought he looked a little better, but as he sat up to drink it, she saw the back of his pyjama top was soaked.

She took the empty cup and brought the juice, placing it on the bedside table. 'Where do you keep clean sheets?' she asked him.

'I don't want clean sheets,' he said wearily.

'Yes, you do. And pyjamas too. In one of these drawers?' She moved over to the long dressing table, and he said, 'Oh, get back to work, and stop playing Florence Nightingale.'

The first drawer held socks and underwear, and she opened the second, found what she wanted, and carried the cream-coloured pyjamas with dark brown piping over to the bed.

'Sheets?' she said.

'There's a cupboard in the kitchen left of the sink.'

She brought them in, and he said, 'Are you going to undress me?'

'I'll help you to the bathroom if you need me to,' she said. 'I suggest you have a bath or shower, if you can manage it, and by the time you've finished I'll have made the bed.'

He threw back the sheet and picked up the fresh pyjamas, thrusting past her proffered hand without looking at her.

She smiled faintly at the slam of the bathroom door and stripped the bed quickly. When he came back, it was freshly made and turned down, and Larissa had put the soiled linen into the washing machine in the small laundry annex off the kitchen and was mixing and heating a packet of chicken soup, cutting thin slices of bread to toast and serve with it.

She brought it to him on a tray, taking note of the straight line of his mouth, and the frown between his hard eyes, but ignoring them. He looked much more comfortable already, and when he had silently finished the soup and half the toast, his skin had lost some of its pallor.

'Had enough?' she queried, as he put the plate back on the tray.

'Yes.' He looked up at her, his expression unfathomable. 'Thanks. Now get those letters and notes back to Miss Collins, will you?'

'I'll call in after work,' she said. 'Unless you're expecting Miss Collins or someone else . . . ?'

'Heavens, no!'

'No one?'

'No one. And not you, either.'

'May I use the key Miss Collins gave me?'

'No. You're not to come back. I told you I can manage.'

She silently gathered up the dishes and took them through to the kitchen. When she came back to collect her things, he seemed to have slipped into a doze. Quietly she left, after phoning for another taxi, and waited on the roadside for it to arrive.

After work she caught a bus, and walked the last few blocks from the stop to Tristan's place. She had 'forgotten' to return the key to Miss Collins, and fortunately had not been asked for it. She let herself in, and then walked across to the bedroom door and tapped on it before walking in.

He was propped up on the pillows, a book in his hand, and his hard blue gaze met hers as she crossed the room.

'You look better,' she said.

'I told you not to come back.'

She picked up the nearly empty jug of fruit juice and took it to the kitchen again for a refill. She had bought some fish and a bunch of fresh parsley on the way, and in half an hour she presented him with a plate of steamed fish and parsley sauce, with thinly cut bread and butter. He ate it, had a cup of tea, and let her straighten his bed. Then he said, 'Now, for heavens sake, go home, girl.'

She picked up the cup and saucer and said, 'When I've washed up. Good night, Mr. Sharpe.'

He caught the tiny smile on her lips and said, 'You're enjoying this, aren't you?'

'What?'

'Seeing me down for once. Being able to bully me.'

The smile widened into a frank grin. 'Yes,' she admitted. 'I think I am. It's a nice change.'

'It won't last.'

'Then I'd better make the most of it while it does.' She laughed as she left him.

The next day she returned the key to Miss Collins and asked if she had heard how Mr. Sharpe was.

'Better, apparently,' the woman told her. 'He said this morning that he expects to be back at work tomorrow.'

'That's good,' Larissa murmured, and wondered how well he really was. After work, she decided to find out.

She had to use the door bell this time, hoping that she wouldn't be getting him out of bed.

He opened the door, fully dressed in casual slacks and a shirt open at the neck. His eyes looked clear and cool, and the sick pallor had receded, though his face had a slightly gaunt look.

'Oh, you *are* better,' she said.

'Disappointed?' He stood back to let her in, and she shook her head.

'If you're all right now, I won't stay,' she said. But as she turned he reached out and took her wrist, drawing her into the room and shutting the door.

'You might as well, now that you're here,' he said. 'I've taken a liking to your cooking. I was just thawing some chicken pieces. Want to take over?'

'I thought you couldn't wait to be well enough to throw me out.'

'Atonement,' he said. 'Stay and share it with me.'

She should have said no, of course. There was

practically nothing the matter with him now; he looked almost normal, and he didn't sound as though he cared, really, whether she stayed or not. But he was standing between her and the door, and he didn't look as though he intended to move.

Larissa shrugged and turned towards the kitchen.

Chapter Four

'Very nice.' Tristan pushed away his plate and leaned back in his chair. 'Where did you learn to cook?'

'I just picked it up.' Larissa took the last mouthful of chicken and put down her fork. 'I didn't make a dessert, but I see you have tinned fruit and ice cream. Do you want some?'

'No, thanks. Get some for yourself if you like.'

She shook her head, gathering up their plates. 'Tea or coffee?'

'Coffee. We'll have it in the other room.'

He helped her to make it and carried the two cups into the lounge, placing them side by side on the low table in front of one of the sofas.

For such an austere-looking room, the sofa was a surprisingly comfortable piece of furniture, the leather softer than it appeared, with a deep foam upholstery underneath it.

He leaned back in the corner, looking at her while he sipped from his cup. 'Do you still intend to leave me?'

For a moment she was at a loss, then she realised he was talking about her leaving her job, and said, 'I haven't really thought about it much. It depends on what comes up.'

'Have you been looking?'

'Not very hard,' she admitted. She looked up and saw the corner of his mouth drawn down. Sensing disapproval, she said, 'Do you want to get rid of me?'

'If I did, I would have done it before now.'

She smiled faintly. He would have, too, she thought.

He put his cup down on the table and said, 'Why did you come back tonight?'

'To see if you were all right,' she said. 'In case you still needed anything.'

'I don't,' he said, with such an odd inflection that she looked at him sharply, puzzled.

'I know.' She placed her cup beside his. 'You're quite recovered.'

'Am I?' he said under his breath, his face turned from her, a hand going briefly behind his neck, then dropping to the back of the sofa. He looked down at her, his mouth wearing a strange, twisted smile. 'You'd have done it for anyone, of course.'

'Yes.' She was uneasy, unable to understand his mood. '*Are* you all right?' she asked uncertainly.

'Yes, of course. Is your flatmate expecting you? You'd better go.'

Chagrin warred with amusement within her. 'You really are the rudest man . . . !' she said. 'I'll do the dishes—'

'No, you won't. Just go, will you?'

'For heavens sake!' she said crossly. 'First you insisted that I stay, now anyone would think you can't stand the sight of me!'

'That's right,' he said. 'I can't.'

Her lips parted, but she couldn't speak. Her throat tightened with suppressed tears, even as she told herself that she hated him, horrible, callous, unfeeling brute that he was.

She made to get up, clumsily, and one of the coffee cups rocked as her hand blindly contacted it. She moved both hands quickly to steady it, and as she let go, Tristan leaned over and pulled her back onto the sofa, his hands gripping her upper arms as he held her close to him.

He saw the brightness of tears in her eyes and said, 'Stop it, you little idiot. Why should that hurt you? You don't care about me—do you?'

For an instant, she glimpsed something behind the hardness of his eyes. Then it was gone, and she groped for an answer. 'I—I don't know,' she said weakly, knowing it was inadequate. 'But you were trying to hurt me—you know you were!'

'So? Maybe I needed to—because I can't stand the sight of you sitting there two feet from me when I want you here, close to me, in my arms.'

He said it quite coolly, without a hint of passion, and she stared and whispered, *'What?'*

'You're becoming an obsession with me,' he told her. 'I want you—quite ridiculously.'

She heard the self-ridicule in his voice and felt his fingers tighten on her shoulders. Some inkling of the control he was exercising got through to her, and she looked at the darkening pupils of his eyes and the faint sheen of perspiration on his forehead and shivered.

'Am I frightening you?' he said.

'I think you are—a little.' Her eyes were wide, fixed on his face, trying to fathom the emotions behind the taut skin, the slightly sadistic twist of his mouth.

'You should have gone when I told you to,' he said. 'When you had a chance.'

'Don't I have a chance any more?' she asked him, her voice shaking.

'Not one.' And a hand moved behind her back to pull her to him, as his head bent and his mouth closed over hers, possessively, determined and still with the faintly cruel edge that she had seen in his smile. But her fear was shot through with a slowly awakening desire, and when she stopped plucking nervously at his sleeve and let her arm slide about his neck, and her lips opened to his passion, the cruelty faded and was replaced by a piercing tenderness. She responded to it with innocent eagerness, and he shifted so that she lay across him, her head cradled against his arm at the end of the sofa, while his other hand began a series of tantalising caresses of her body, making her shiver with pleasure. He touched her breast lightly and she drew a sharp breath, so that the swelling mound rose against his hand, and he closed his fingers over it as his kiss became deeper and more urgent.

He raised his head, and she felt a tiny spurt of triumph when she saw that his eyes were brilliant and narrowed, and heard his quickened breathing. His mouth sought her throat and burned through her dress over her breast, and she watched with half-closed eyes, and pushed her fingers into his hair, feeling the amazing softness of it, ruffling it so that the electric light burnished the separate strands to gold.

Her hand slipped to his neck, and she tentatively pushed her fingers inside the collar of his shirt, feeling the ridge of his spine, the warmth and slight dampness of his skin. He moved and buried his lips in the smooth skin of her neck, and she felt his hand behind her, pulling at the zipper that fastened her dress.

It stuck, and he moved to free it with both hands, his weight suddenly heavy on her as he turned, and she realised that she was lying almost full-length on the sofa now. The zip moved, and his hand slid the dress forward to bare a shoulder to the warm caress of his mouth. She felt the cool air on her back where her dress was open, and the miasma of passion that had held her began to clear. The coldness spread, and when his lips moved lower, his hand pulling down her dress to give him her breast, she suddenly went rigid and gasped, 'Tristan?'

At the questioning note, he raised his head, his eyes coming back to rest on her face. He saw the desperate pleading in her eyes, and when she gasped his name again, he went very still, his hands still holding her. She saw his eyes harden, and the mask descend again over his face. He said, 'Well?'

Her hand fumbled anxiously at her dress, covering the lacy bra and the bared skin above it. He watched the movement coldly and then returned his eyes to her face. 'You don't want it,' he said flatly, a thread of bitter amusement behind the flatness.

'I—I'm not sure,' she whispered miserably. 'I'm not sure enough.'

He raised an eyebrow, and sat up, pulling her with him and sliding up her zipper in a swift, easy movement. 'Sure of what?' he said. 'Me? Yourself?'

His arm was still across her shoulders, and he took her chin in his other hand and raised her face to his. 'Both,' she said shakily. 'I don't know what you— what you really feel about me—and I don't know what my own feelings mean.'

'Haven't you ever wanted a man before?' His tone was a shade derisory, and she flushed as she said baldly, 'No.'

'And now you do, and you don't know what to do about it.'

He released her suddenly and stood up, pacing away from her across the room.

'I suppose it seems very simple to you,' she said. 'I should just go to bed with you—and you'd be the first of—who knows how many? The trouble is, that isn't how I want to live my life. I've had too many temporary relationships already. I don't want a series of love affairs. I want one man—one love.'

He had turned to look at her from several paces away. 'That's how you've planned your life?' he asked her.

'Yes.'

She was looking down at her hands, tightly clenched in her lap. He said, 'Do you have a candidate in mind?'

'No. There's plenty of time.'

'You haven't got a boyfriend?'

'I go out with boys—men. But there's no one special. There never has been.'

'And you weren't interested in the—"position"—that I offered you earlier.'

'You withdrew the offer.'

'So I did. Were you disappointed?'

'I think I was relieved.'

'Why?'

'Because,' she said slowly, 'I would have found it difficult to make the decision.'

'I'll give you an easier one.' He paused, and then said, 'Would you marry me, Larissa?'

She had no words to answer him. It was a fantastic suggestion, and for a moment or two she doubted that she had heard right. Eventually, she stammered, her voice high with disbelief, 'That's *easier?*'

'Don't you think so? That *is* what you meant by *one man, one love,* wasn't it?'

'Yes. But I wasn't thinking of *you* as the man.'

'I'm the only man you've ever wanted,' he said, the mocking note strong in his voice. 'You just admitted it.'

Larissa got to her feet, jerkily. 'That isn't necessarily love,' she said.

'Infatuation?' he suggested dryly.

She considered that; she had to. 'No,' she said. 'I'm not infatuated with you.'

He smiled slightly, and she said, 'What about you? You said that I'm an "obsession" with you. Is that love? Do you love me, Tristan?'

'The age-old female question,' he said ironically. 'Do I love you?' He looked at her, and if there was any expression on his face, she would have guessed it was dislike. But he said, 'All right, my dear. I love you. Now, do I get an answer?'

'Can't I have some time to think about it?' she said uncertainly. She tried a shaky smile. 'You sound more like an employer than a lover.'

He made an impatient movement and came over to where she stood, pushing her chin up with his hand. The hard line of his mouth altered slightly then. He said softly, 'Don't look so scared; I'm only going to kiss you—like a lover.'

As his mouth touched hers his hand slid around to her nape, holding her head at the angle that he wanted, and his other hand pulled her against him. This time there was only gentleness and a devastating expertise that made her dizzy with longing for delights she had never experienced. She touched his sleeve, clutched at it to keep her balance, because the world was spinning about her, his mouth the centre of a vortex of sensation, draining her, taking her over, and his hands when they began to caress her slim body created tiny ripples of excitement that gathered into an overwhelming wave.

It was all too much, and she gave a low whimper of bewilderment and jerked her head aside to lay her forehead against his shoulder, gasping and still clinging to him.

His hand smoothed her hair, his thumb pushing a tumbled strand behind her ear and moving gently on her cheek. His fingers stroked her spine, absently caressing. 'Well?' he said quietly against her temple.

She gulped a little, and whispered, 'I love you.'

'Of course.'

He sounded very ironic, and she didn't know if it was directed at her, or himself. But when she moved her head, trying to look at his face, his hand on her hair kept her face against his shoulder. Then he said, 'So?' and began pressing brief, gentle kisses on her temple, moving down to her cheek. His restraining hand slid to her shoulder, and she lifted her face to his mouth, her eyes closed, loving the soft touch of his lips on her eyelids, in the hollow behind her ear, along the curve of her jawline. She turned her lips to his, seekingly, and with his mouth barely touching hers, he said, 'Are you going to marry me?'

'Yes,' she whispered, and felt him go very still for an instant, before his mouth opened hers beneath it and swept her back into the vivid, lightning-shot whirlpool of passion.

It was he who put the brake on this time, quite suddenly pushing her away, his hands so tight on her arms that she winced. She was trembling, scarcely aware of what she was doing, only brilliantly conscious of what he had been doing to her.

When she looked at him with dazed eyes, his face was tautly controlled, and his eyes flickered over her with a knowledge, almost a contempt, that made her dig her teeth into her lower lip and tense every muscle in an effort to hide the devastating effect he had on her.

The faint, cynical smile touching his mouth told her she was unsuccessful, but when she made a slight movement of escape, he let her go.

She backed away from him, suppressing the temptation to rub her arms where he had held them, and raised shaking fingers to her hair, attempting to smooth it into order.

'You're not doing much good,' he commented. 'Do you want a comb?'

'There's one in my bag,' she said, looking about for it. He handed it to her from a table by the door, and she combed her hair and applied some lipstick to her still-throbbing mouth, turning her back to him.

'I'll take you home,' he said.

'No, don't. You've been sick—'

'I'm coming back to work tomorrow. What's the difference?'

'If you'd just call me a taxi—'

'I'm not putting you in a taxi tonight. I'll get a jacket.'

His voice was curt, and when he came out of the bedroom, shrugging into a jacket, she searched his face and he looked back at her unsmilingly. As the car moved smoothly through the streets she fixed her eyes on the windscreen, watching the pole houses and new bungalows give way to tall narrow colonials and then the high-rise buildings of the city before they skirted the harbour and eventually arrived in her quiet suburban street.

She felt strangely let down, almost depressed, her eyes stinging with unaccountable tears. She blinked hard and swallowed, and although he hadn't looked at her, Tristan's hand suddenly descended warmly on hers where it lay in her lap, and held it tightly.

The contact comforted her, and when he drew up outside her home, and removed his hand from hers, she missed it.

He didn't linger, merely opened her door and went with her up the shallow flight of steps, waited for her to fit her key in the latch, and then turned her face to his for a brief, hard kiss.

The lights were on, and Sharon, her flatmate, was curled up in an armchair in the living room, reading a paperback romance while she waved a portable drier over her newly washed hair. Larissa glanced at the clock and realised that it wasn't late at all. She had been with Tristan for less than two hours.

Sharon looked up and pressed the off button on the drier, and said, 'Hi! Where've you been? Have you eaten?'

Larissa blinked. The light seemed very bright, and Sharon's cheerful voice and ordinary, attractively freckled face brought a sudden breath of normality into what had until now been a fantastic evening. 'Yes,' she said. 'I've eaten.'

'Alone?' Sharon asked curiously.

Larissa looked at her for a minute, until the question penetrated. 'No,' she said. 'With Tristan.'

'The boss?'

Larissa nodded.

'Kept you working late again, did he?' Sharon asked. 'If you ask me, he's a slave driver. Still, if he feeds you well . . . *I* had beans on toast.'

She switched on the drier again and raised it to her hair. Then, seeing Larissa still standing just inside the door, she frowned and turned it off once more. 'Hey, are you all right?' she asked. 'Did he make a pass or something?'

Larissa came slowly into the centre of the room and dropped her bag onto a chair. Perhaps if she put it into words she would lose this disconcerting feeling of unreality. 'I suppose you could call it "or something," she said uncertainly. 'He asked me to marry him. And I said yes.'

'He—*what?* You *did?*' Sharon's candid blue eyes widened, and the drier dropped from her hand to her lap. 'Good heavens!' she said weakly. 'I didn't think he was the type. I mean, from what you've said about him, I thought he was a cold fish.'

'He is,' Larissa said involuntarily. Then she stammered, 'At least—I thought—'

She stopped, flushing, and Sharon said, 'Uh-huh. A dark horse, is he? You want to watch him, Larry.'

Her smile was teasing, but her eyes held a slight anxiety. 'You never said anything.'

'I didn't know. . . .'

'That he was in love with you? Or that you were in love with him?' Sharon paused, her head tilted suddenly to one side, a frown between her carefully shaped brows. 'You *are* in love with him, aren't you?'

'Yes . . . I think so.'

'*Larry!* You only *think so?*'

'I've never been in love before,' Larissa confessed. She sat down on the chair beside her friend and said, 'You're supposed to know, when it happens, aren't you? You're supposed to be sure.'

'Is *he* sure?' Sharon asked bluntly.

'I don't think he's ever been unsure of anything in his life. He says . . . I'm an obsession.'

Sharon's feelings showed in her face, awe struggling with unease. 'Don't let him rush you into anything,' she said seriously. 'And I mean *anything!*'

Larissa smiled faintly. 'He hasn't tried to get me into bed, Sharon,' she said frankly. 'He could have, tonight. But he didn't.'

'I'm glad. You're not the type.'

'No, I'm not. I told him that.'

'Is that why he proposed?' Sharon asked bluntly.

'I don't know. If it is, it's not a very good reason, is it?'

'Not if it's the only reason. Sex without love . . . It doesn't last, does it?'

'How do we know, Sharon?' Larissa asked.

An odd expression of bitterness crossed Sharon's face. Then she faced her friend squarely and said quietly, '*I* know!'

Surprise held Larissa silent for a moment. 'Sharon . . . ?' she said.

Sharon nodded grimly. 'You just be careful,' she said. 'Men will sell their souls for sex.'

'Sharon!'

'Well, they will—most of them. And you're much too nice to be hurt. Come to think of it,' she added, with a return to her normal cheerful manner, 'why am I worrying? Of course the guy's head over heels for you. You're sweet as well as sexy, and as brainy as you're beautiful. Why shouldn't he love you? He'd be mad not to.'

'Thanks for the testimonial,' Larissa said, smiling. 'I'll have to introduce you to him.'

'Yes, you will,' Sharon agreed, rather abruptly. Then, 'Hey, have we got some of that sherry left we bought for the trifle when Carol and Malcolm came to dinner? We should be drinking a toast to your engagement.'

The introduction, when it came, was less than successful. Tristan called for Larissa, having arranged for them to have dinner with his mother, who had flown from Christchurch expressly to meet her. Larissa, nervous about the meeting, had changed her mind twice about what to wear, and was still trying to arrange her hair in a new and more sophisticated style when Tristan's peremptory knock fell on the door.

Sharon, hovering with hairpins and advice, said, 'Don't worry, I'll look after him until you're ready. Take your time; he's two minutes early, anyway.'

Larissa didn't take her time, she hurried, with the result that the hairstyle was a disaster, and she ended up doing it all over again. The finished product was satisfactory this time, though, and she hoped Tristan would approve. She could hear the murmur of voices in the living room, but not what was being said, and when she closed the bedroom door and started down the short passageway in her high-heeled sandals, the sudden silence seemed strained.

As she stood in the doorway her heart sank.

Sharon was looking flushed and self-conscious, her eyes angry, and Tristan stood near the door, patently waiting to go, one hand in his pocket, and his face tight and cold.

She moved into the room and said evenly, 'I'm sorry I kept you waiting, Tristan. You and Sharon have introduced yourselves, I suppose?'

'Yes,' he said. 'Are you ready, now?'

She cast Sharon a glance which the other girl returned with a wry and rather shaky grin, and went across to him. She said good night to Sharon, adding, 'I won't be late,' and heard Tristan give her a curt 'Good night' before he closed the door behind them.

In the car, she said, 'Sharon's my best friend.'

'So I gather.'

'Why did you snub her?'

He didn't deny it. 'If you must exchange girlish confidences, she should learn to keep them to herself.'

'She wouldn't betray my confidence,' Larissa said with certainty. 'What did she say to annoy you?'

'Specifically? Very little. Between the lines, I gather I'm the big bad wolf who's all set to gobble up Red Riding Hood. I take it she's the one who talked you into a longer engagement.'

'She didn't talk me into anything,' Larissa said steadily.

'She said she'd advised you to make it longer than the couple of months that I suggested—'

'Yes, she did, but I didn't have to take her advice.'

'You'll oblige me by refraining from discussing our relationship with your friend in future,' he said with chilly formality.

Larissa opened her lips on a furious retort, twisting in her seat to face him, and then suddenly giggled, her hand going to her mouth. When he turned his head in quick, frowning surprise, she said 'You sound as though you're dictating a memo!'

His foot hit the brake, bringing the car to an abrupt halt under a street lamp. He turned to her and his hand shot out to curve about her nape and pull her close. His mouth came down hard on her lips, stifling the laughter that still parted them, setting her pulses racing crazily. Then she was freed with equal suddenness, and he started the car again without a word.

Larissa sat beside him, stunned into silence. She didn't know if the kiss had been a punishment for laughing at him or precipitated by an emotion other than anger. Her lips stung, and she nervously touched her tongue to them. Her hand went to her hair, checking the pins and the carefully arranged knot at her nape, just above where his fingers had held her, almost bruising against the smooth skin. He had said nothing about the new style; perhaps he had not even noticed.

When they arrived at the hotel where his mother was staying, he guided her towards one of the lounges, and as her fingers again went to her hair he swept a glance over her, taking in the simply styled cream dress with a gold chain belt and plain round neckline, and the soft dark hair drawn back from her face and secured with pins and a tortoiseshell ornamental comb.

'Don't be nervous,' he said, and she dropped her hand hastily, imagining disapproval in his tone, his glance.

He took the hand in a warm, hard grasp and raised his other hand to fleetingly touch her cheek. He gave her one of his rare smiles, and she realised he was trying to be reassuring, and smiled back.

His mother was waiting for them, a tall blond woman with disillusioned eyes and smooth pale skin, an exquisite figure set off by a superbly cut black dress, and a very expensive-looking fur about her shoulders.

'How nice to meet you, Larissa,' she said, when Tristan had introduced them. Her hand was cool as she briefly touched Larissa's, her smile equally so. And the blue eyes looked interested but unimpressed.

'I'm very pleased to meet you, too, Mrs. Sharpe,' Larissa said politely. She added, 'Tristan is very like you.'

'Is he?' She sounded amused, turning to her son. 'Should I take it as a compliment, do you think, Tristan?'

'Take it as it was meant,' he advised lazily. 'She *has* promised to marry me.'

They *are* alike, Larissa thought. Not only in looks. There was a definite similarity of manner, too. They understood each other, these two, and there were several moments during dinner when Larissa felt an outsider as obliquely pointed remarks flowed between Tristan and his mother. She wondered about his father. He had told her his parents were divorced, and when she had said, 'I'm sorry. That must have been hard for you,' he had returned, 'Don't be sorry. It was the best thing that ever happened for all of us.' His father had remarried, he said, and they rarely saw each other. But his mother wanted to meet Larissa.

'Larissa Lovegrove,' Mrs. Sharpe said, stirring her coffee thoughtfully. 'I wondered if Tristan was serious when he first told me. Such a very pretty name. *Too pretty to be true,* her eyes said, with all her son's mockery.

'Her flatmate calls her Larry,' Tristan murmured acidly, his eyes mirroring his mother's.

'It amuses Tristan, too,' Larissa said. 'Where did

Tristan get his name, Mrs. Sharpe? It's unusual, surely?'

'Oh, his father was a romantic,' she said with scarcely veiled contempt. 'He was conceived on our honeymoon, within sight of Tristan da Cunha—we were on a cruise ship. At least, that's when Gerald liked to believe it happened. Romantic people always prefer their own version of the facts.'

With a slight smile, Larissa asked, 'Weren't you ever romantic, Mrs. Sharpe?'

Something flickered for an instant in the hard eyes. Then the discreetly made-up lids fell, and Mrs. Sharpe said, 'If I was, it's so long ago I've forgotten.' In the same bored tone, she went on, 'And for heavens sake, call me Helen, child. I hope you don't have any yearning to call me *Mother*. Being a mother-in-law is a daunting enough prospect without that!'

Larissa, who had vaguely looked forward to acquiring a surrogate family when she married, said steadily, 'I don't think you're anyone's idea of a mother-in-law, Mrs. Sharpe—I'm sorry—Helen.'

'Thank heaven!' The sleek blond head tipped back as she drained her coffee, and Larissa met Tristan's unsmiling, narrowed glance across the table with a certain defiance.

Helen took out a slim gold cigarette case and lighter. Larissa shook her head at the offer of a smoke, and Tristan took the lighter and without comment waited for his mother to fit a cigarette into a slim black holder, and lit it for her.

'Of course, you don't smoke,' she said to Larissa, in her light, amused voice. 'If you did, Tristan would have broken you of it by now.' She blew smoke through pursed lips, tipping her head back, and laughed. 'He's given up trying to influence me, I'm glad to say. What a boring little prig you were as a teenager, darling!' she added, slanting him a glance across the table.

'Aren't we all?' he said lightly.

'Aren't you forgetting that you're marrying one?' she asked, with slightly malicious pleasure. 'You did tell me that Larissa is only nineteen, didn't you?'

'She's the exception.'

'The one that proves the rule? How trite of you, Tristan.'

Larissa saw the tightening of his mouth, and some instinct made her put her hand over his, where it lay on the table.

He glanced quickly at her and then away, and his hand turned under hers and clasped it in a grip that almost hurt.

'What a couple of lovebirds!' his mother said indulgently. Blue smoke veiled her eyes as she looked at their entwined hands. But there was sharp mockery in her face as she looked up and said, 'There must be something of your father in you, after all, Tristan.'

Larissa felt Tristan's fingers momentarily tighten further on hers. Then his grip relaxed a little and he said quietly, 'I hope so.'

She raised her eyes to look at him and saw his eyes fixed with cold remorselessness on his mother's face. Helen was trying to smile, but her teeth were clenched and her thin, carefully reddened lips trembled. She put the black holder to her mouth and drew deeply, removing it with a peculiarly uncoordinated little wave of her hand.

Larissa saw the effort with which she wrenched her eyes from Tristan's. Then, with a strange, bitter little laugh, she said, 'Well, you've certainly got yourself a man, Larissa, dear. I'll be invited to the wedding, I hope. They're not really my scene these days, but after all, when the groom is my only son . . .'

'Of course you'll be invited,' Larissa said warmly, distressed by the undercurrents she sensed, without understanding them. 'We both want you there.'

Helen had recovered her poise very quickly. She glanced at Tristan's impassive face and raised her brows. 'Do you? That's very sweet of you, Larissa.' She took a last draw on her cigarette and said, 'You'll be wearing white, of course. It means nothing these days; you girls are all so liberated, aren't you? But oh, to be young again, in a white bridal gown with all my illusions intact! Among other things.'

'That's enough!' Tristan said, icily.

She carefully removed her cigarette from the holder to daintily put it out in the glass ashtray on the table. 'Sorry, darling,' she drawled. 'Am I embarrassing your fiancée? Frankly, I didn't think it was possible nowadays to embarrass the young!'

'I'm not embarrassed,' Larissa said quietly.

Helen stared at her as though she was an interesting and hitherto unknown species. 'This child has manners, too!' she said. 'What a quaint upbringing you must have had.'

'I told you about Larissa's background,' Tristan's hard voice said.

'Oh, yes, of course. You have no people, have you? I suppose that's why Tristan appeals to you—a father figure?' Her inimical eyes went to Tristan. 'And I don't need three guesses to know why you appeal to *him*.' Her gaze flickered back to Larissa's face. 'You really are extremely pretty,' she said sincerely. 'And with the freshness that only youth can give a girl. I'm sure it's an irresistible combination for a man.'

'If you've finished—' Tristan said, rising and pushing back his chair, 'Larissa doesn't want to be late.'

'For bed?' Helen asked archly, and laughed. Tristan held Larissa's chair as she rose, then came round to do the same for his mother. 'Yes, do see that she gets her beauty sleep,' she cooed, turning to smile at him. 'It's important at her age.' Then she said admiringly as he replaced the fur she had slipped over the back of her chair, 'You do that with such panache! I must say you've matured beautifully, Tristan. You've no idea, Larissa, what a frightfully graceless adolescent he was. Sullen, too. I'm constantly surprised that he grew up even half-civilised. Now *your* generation seems to have been born with poise!'

Tristan said, in the thoroughly bored tones that Larissa was beginning to know, 'Don't you think you've harped on that theme long enough? Larissa's hardly of a different generation from me.'

His mother laughed delightedly. 'Don't be so touchy, Tristan! You mustn't mind a little teasing! Take me into the bar, and I'll buy you a drink,' she added coaxingly.

'You know very well that Larissa isn't allowed in the bar,' Tristan said, very dry.

Helen grimaced. 'Put my foot in it again, have I? Well, all right, then. I'll retire to my room and let you two children go along. I expect you can't wait to be alone. It was nice meeting you, Larissa.'

Larissa smelled her expensive, musky perfume as she bent to kiss the air somewhere near the girl's cheek, then turned to her son. 'Good night, Tristan. Oh, and congratulations. She's lovely, of course. And no doubt she'll adore you if you treat her right. Don't grow too like your father!'

When the car stopped outside her flat, Larissa found that her hands were clenched, and her back ached from tension. Tristan said flatly, 'I'm sorry I let you in for that. She isn't usually as bad as she was tonight.'

'She's very unhappy, isn't she?'

'And very jealous.'

'Jealous? Over you?'

'Me?' He sounded derisive. 'It's nothing to do with me. She's never been the doting type of mother. She's jealous of youth and beauty, that's all. That's what attracted my father to her. And when he left her, it was to go to a much younger woman.'

'She could still be very attractive, if . . .'

'Yes, *if*. If she stopped thinking of herself as my father's discarded wife. If she'd make a new life for herself instead of constantly harping on the wreckage of her marriage. If she'd ever had anything more than her beauty and her youth with which to attract a man.'

'You weren't very kind to her, were you? Tonight, I mean.'

'Did you want me to be? When she was sharpening her claws on you?'

She hesitated. 'Were you protecting me?'

'Yes, I suppose I was. Surprised?'

'I am, a bit.'

'Why? Because I'm not above being unkind to you myself, on occasion?'

'They haven't been very frequent,' she said. 'But I don't like you to be cruel to your mother. I'm sorry for her.'

'For having such an unnatural son? No need, I assure you. Funny thing, she's actually liked me much better since I stopped trying to please her. When I was younger I could never do a damned thing right, anyway.'

He said it lightly, a throwaway line, and she could only guess what past hurts lay behind it. '*You* haven't been happy, either, have you?' she said, gropingly.

'Soft as butter, aren't you?' he scoffed. 'I don't want your pity, Larissa.'

'It isn't pity, it's sympathy.'

'Whatever it is, don't waste it. I'm not in need of it.'

'Are you ever in need of anything?' He seemed the most totally self-sufficient person she had ever known.

'That's a very provocative question,' he said. 'Was it meant to be?'

'No, it was meant to be serious.'

But he evidently didn't want to be serious. 'After an evening with my mother,' he said, 'what's needed is a little light relief! Come here.'

His lovemaking was light and almost teasingly restrained, leaving her pleasantly tingling and vaguely regretful when he moved away from her and opened the door of the car.

He kissed her more deeply on the doorstep, until she trembled in his arms and pressed herself blindly against him. After he had gone, she let herself in and Sharon took one look at her and blushed, glancing away.

'How was it?' she asked, very casual. 'What's his mother like?'

'All right,' Larissa said. 'She's very like him.'

'There can't be two of them!' Sharon said flippantly. She looked at Larissa again, and said quickly, 'Sorry, that was pretty crass, wasn't it?'

'It's all right. I know you didn't hit it off with Tristan.' She would have liked to talk about the evening, Tristan's peculiar relationship with his mother, and get Sharon's opinion. But Tristan's biting request not to discuss him with her friend inhibited her. 'The dinner was super,' she said instead, and launched into a stilted description of what they had eaten.

Sharon made 'yummy' noises, and pretended envy, but when Larissa had finished her culinary report, a strained little silence fell.

Eventually, Sharon said brightly, 'What did he think of your hairstyle?'

'He didn't say.'

'Men!' Sharon grimaced. 'You spend hours prinking for them, and they don't even notice.'

But Tristan would have noticed, Larissa thought. He never missed a detail like that. Perhaps he didn't like it. As he had made no comment, she wouldn't wear it that way again.

Chapter Five

At work, her engagement ring set her apart. She had
expected surprise at first, but she had not realised
that being Tristan's fiancée would put an unbridge-
able distance between her and the rest of the staff.
The young men looked sheepish when they came
through reception and saw her at the desk, and she
knew they were recalling the days when they had
entered into a friendly conspiracy and wondering
how close she had been to Tristan then. Miss Collins
managed to convey disapproval without deviating in
the slightest from her usual efficient manner, and the
other typists tempered their former friendliness with
a new restraint in conversation in case they let slip an
uncomplimentary remark about the boss.

In the office, Tristan's manner towards her was the
same as it had always been, and when she tried, one
weekend, to tell him how difficult she felt her
position was, he seemed coldly surprised that it
bothered her and faintly bored that she should think
it worth telling him about. Larissa faltered into
silence. Perhaps aware that he had failed her in some
way, he said brusquely, 'It isn't for long, anyway.

Once we're married, you can kiss the office good-bye. In fact, you could leave before then, if you like.'

'You mean you don't want a working wife?'

'I certainly don't need one. Are you one of those women who feel unfulfilled if they're not earning a wage packet?'

'I don't know. I've scarcely had time to find out.'

His eyes went colder than ever and he said, 'I don't want you working for me, anyway. If you get bored at home, we can discuss the matter when it arises.'

'Are we going to live in your flat?'

'Not if you don't like it.'

'It's all right,' she said hastily. 'But very masculine. A house would be nice later, don't you think?'

'Later?'

'Well . . . if we start a family.'

She looked away from the sardonic gleam in his eyes.

'Do you want children?' he said softly, and she managed to look at him squarely and say, 'Don't you?'

They had been out walking and were seated side by side on a wooden bench, looking out over the city. She wore jeans and a cotton shirt, and the nippy Wellington breeze had tangled her hair into unruly curls. His eyes slipped over her, and he said, 'You're barely more than a child yourself. Don't you think it's early days to be talking of having a family?'

'If I'm old enough to be married, I'm old enough to have children,' she said stubbornly.

His mouth curled unpleasantly, and he said, under his breath, 'That's the whole damned trouble!'

Larissa jumped up and cried angrily, 'If you think I'm such a baby, why did you ask me to marry you? What are you? Some kind of pervert?'

He got to his feet, much less speedily and with

more grace, and looked down at her. 'Possibly,' he said.

'Oh, don't be so *idiotic!*' Larissa snapped, making him raise his brows. 'I'll be twenty before you know it.'

'I live for the day.'

She cast him an exasperated glance and turned away, walking quickly in the direction they had come from. He was soon striding beside her, and as the path wound uphill she became breathless and had to slow her pace.

Perhaps as a peace offering, he said, 'If you want to redecorate the flat, you can.'

'I wouldn't dare!'

'What's that supposed to mean?' he enquired frostily.

'You've obviously paid a very expensive interior decorator to do it for you. I'd probably fill it with pink satin pillows and teddy bears.'

'I doubt it.'

'You mean you'd actually trust my judgement?'

His hand descended firmly on her arm, and he stopped walking, holding her there. 'I don't give a damn if your taste runs to pink satin and teddy bears,' he said evenly. 'You can do what you like with the place.'

'Supposing you hate my taste?' she demanded. 'It might drive you crazy!'

'So might you,' he said softly. 'But I want you there.'

She looked at him uncertainly, trying to gauge his expression. 'Joke?' she said, trying a smile.

'No joke.'

'I don't understand you,' she said. 'Why me?'

'Perhaps because you'll probably drive me crazy,' he said ironically.

'Oh, you're a masochist!' she said lightly, surprising him into a crack of laughter.

'That must be it,' he said blandly. 'Satisfied?'

She wasn't. Somehow he had deflected both her anger and her anxiety. He was never exactly a comfortable companion, but in this mood he was a stimulating one. She found him frequently baffling and quite often annoyingly enigmatic when she was seething with emotion, but he never bored her.

He took her to see an exhibition of paintings by a friend of his. They were very abstract, and she found them frankly puzzling, but Tristan introduced her to the artist, and as he talked about his work she began to understand what he was trying to convey. She also realised that Tristan knew quite a lot about the subject, and when she showed interest he lent her books on art and took her to more exhibitions, patiently explaining the finer points and apparently listening with respect to her hesitant opinions, encouraging her to express them.

Surprised, she said, once, 'I thought you'd scoff at my ideas.'

'Why should you think that?'

'Well . . . you can be very crushing when you think I've said something stupid.'

'Only when you *have* said something stupid.'

'In your opinion?' she said, her eyes dancing with challenge.

'All right. In my opinion. You've never looked crushed.'

'How do I look, then?'

'Militant, usually, when I've annoyed you.'

'You do it on purpose, don't you?' she said thoughtfully. 'Annoy me.'

'Occasionally. Not without good reason.'

'What constitutes a good reason, then?'

He didn't answer for a moment. Then he said, 'The pleasure of watching you simmer, perhaps. It makes your eyes brighten beautifully.'

Larissa grimaced. 'Why don't you just tell me I'm pretty when I'm mad?' she said disgustedly.

'Because, one, it's a very hackneyed line, and two, you already know it.'

'You never get mad, do you?' she mused. 'Icily angry, but not red-hot mad.' She regarded him steadily, wondering what it would take. . . .

And then Tristan looked up and saw the speculation in her face. 'Don't try it,' he said. 'You wouldn't enjoy it.'

Larissa dropped her eyes, a shiver running down her spine. He hadn't been fooling. If he ever did lose his temper, it would be wise to be a very long way away.

Sharon and Tristan had never got over their initial antagonism. Although her friend was reluctant to mention Tristan at all, Larissa could hardly be unaware of the concern with which Sharon viewed her engagement. It made the atmosphere in the flat a little strained at times, and once, when Sharon did speak out, unable to bottle up her misgivings any longer, they came close to quarrelling.

Larissa was distressed by it, and she asked Tristan if he would make a foursome one evening with Sharon and her current boyfriend, and try to be friendly.

His eyes cool and distant, he said, 'Is it important to you?'

'Yes, it is.' She wouldn't plead with him. She waited quietly, and he shrugged and said, 'Very well. Dinner and dancing, or a show and supper afterwards?'

'Sharon enjoys dancing,' she said eagerly. 'Thank you, Tristan.'

'Thank me properly,' he said, and she leaned over and kissed him. His lips remained unresponsive, and she drew back, disconcerted. He was watching her, and she was chilled by the coolly assessing gaze.

Then he put his hands on her arms and drew her towards him, kissed her thoroughly and pushed her gently away. She felt the heat in her cheeks, the spreading warmth throughout her entire body, and resented the fact that he looked composed, unmoved. It was always like that, she thought confusedly. Whenever he kissed her he seemed to be clinically interested in her reactions, studying the effect he had on her, but of his feelings she knew nothing. There might be a slightly faster rhythm to his breathing, or an occasional darkening glitter in the blue eyes, but that was all. He could reduce her to inarticulate, breathless longing, and then draw back and start talking about the weather or business as though nothing had taken place between them.

The evening with Sharon and Dennis was not wildly successful. Dennis was in disgrace with Sharon, after a skirmish at the door of the flat a few nights previously, and in the back of the car they conducted a low-voiced but apparently acrimonious discussion as Tristan drove them to their destination, while Larissa sat beside him tongue-tied simply by the urgent necessity of finding conversation to cover the contretemps going on behind them.

The dinner was undoubtedly superb, but Dennis drank a little too much of the excellent wines Tristan ordered. The reason was presumably Sharon's notably offhand manner, but Larissa was fairly certain that Sharon would have relented very shortly if only Dennis had been prepared to accept a little coolness for a while. But as the wine made him sullen, Sharon became slightly waspish. And Tristan, very urbane but alternately bored or rather maliciously amused by his companions, made matters considerably worse.

It was a relief to leave the table with Tristan when

he asked her to dance, but she held herself stiffly in his arms because she knew the evening was rapidly becoming a disaster, and, perhaps unfairly, felt that he could have exerted himself to prevent it.

'Your friend still doesn't like me,' he observed.

She couldn't refute that. Sharon had made a few clumsy attempts at conversation with Tristan, and he hadn't snubbed her, but Larissa knew very well that the ironic glint with which he watched both Sharon and Dennis had nettled her friend, and that the last few glances she had cast in Tristan's direction had been unmistakably hostile.

'You haven't tried to make her like you,' Larissa said.

'I never try to make people like me,' he answered. 'You should know that.'

She did, of course. 'I thought you might have, this time,' she said. 'For my sake.'

'I arranged this evening for your sake. I don't try to make people *dis*like me, either, you know. I don't believe in putting on an act, that's all. If they like the way I am, okay. If I pretend to be something I'm not, they're going to find that out, sooner or later, and be disappointed.'

'Sharon's worried about me,' she said. 'I hoped to reassure her. I wanted you to get along.'

'Unlikely,' he said. 'She isn't a bit reassured, and she'll try to interfere. Don't listen to her, Larissa.'

'She isn't a troublemaker.'

'Not intentionally, no. She has your best interests at heart. The trouble is, she may not know what those interests really are.'

'Do *you*?'

His slight, cynical smile barely curved his mouth. 'I know what mine are, anyway.'

'You're pretty frank, aren't you?' she said. 'Maybe I *should* listen to Sharon.'

'You do and I'll break her in little bits,' he said.

She stopped dancing, shocked into immobility. Because he had meant it—there had been no humour in his voice, no lightness at all. Her head jerked up. 'Tristan! For heavens sake!'

He wasn't taking anything back. His eyes were hard and steady. She shook her head in disbelief, and shivered.

The music had stopped, other couples jostled them making their way off the floor, and Tristan put his hand on her waist and took her back to their table.

The other two had been dancing, too, but a glance told Larissa it had not improved the situation. Sharon was tight-lipped, and Dennis looked flushed, his chin held at a belligerent angle.

Larissa and Sharon exchanged a few remarks while the men sat silent, and then the music started up again, and Dennis got to his feet and asked Larissa to dance.

Tristan said icily, 'I think not. Larissa's had enough dancing tonight.'

She got up and went on to the floor with Dennis. He held her closely with both arms about her, and his hands were inclined to wander. He was not quite steady on his feet, and his heavy body seemed to lean on her. She glanced at the table, saw Tristan lean slightly forward to speak to Sharon, and Sharon shake her head. Tristan looked up, and for a moment his eyes found hers, before Dennis turned in a stumbling fashion, and she couldn't see him any more. She was terribly conscious, though, that he was watching her all the time she was on the floor. Watching with eyes that were coldly, viciously angry.

There was no point in staying after that, and by mutual consent they left when Dennis and Larissa returned to the table.

Tristan dropped Dennis off first, and then drove them swiftly to the girls' flat.

Sharon must have had her hand on the doorlatch before they stopped. The engine hadn't died before she was out of the car, calling, 'Good night, Tristan. Thanks a lot!' and scooting swiftly up the steps.

Larissa would have liked to follow with equal speed, but Tristan had a firm hold on her wrist.

He said, 'At least your friend knows that three's a crowd.'

Larissa, who had a strong suspicion that Sharon was going to burst into tears as soon as she got inside, pulled at her captured wrist and said, 'I think she's miserable. She quarrelled with Dennis—'

'I did notice. She'll probably scratch your eyes out if you go in now.'

'Of course she won't! Why on earth should she?'

'Isn't it obvious? Her boyfriend thoroughly enjoyed dancing with you—if you could call what you were doing dancing.'

'He probably wanted to make her jealous,' Larissa admitted. 'He was using me.'

'He certainly was—in more ways than one,' Tristan agreed, making her face burn in the darkness. 'And you? Why were you so eager to be used?'

'Why do you put it like that?' she asked angrily. 'It sounds horrible!' She tried again to free her hand, but he ignored her struggles.

'Why did you insist on dancing with him?' Tristan said implacably. 'I gave you an out—you refused to take it.'

'I was *sorry* for him, that's all!'

'Sorry for him! Is that all it takes to make you let a drunken lout paw you in public?'

'I didn't! He wasn't!'

'You did, and he was! I was watching, remember? He was all over you!'

She heard the cold contempt in his voice and said, 'I wasn't trying to make *you* jealous, Tristan.'

'Maybe you don't need to try.' He jerked suddenly on her wrist, pulling her towards him, his body turned so that she was trapped against the seat by him. 'If you want to be held,' he said, 'if you want to be touched, ask *me* for it, not another girl's half-drunk boyfriend.'

His hands were on her as he spoke, making an insolent exploration in a hateful, more explicit parody of the way Dennis's hands had roamed while they were dancing.

'Don't!' she choked. 'I didn't want it! I didn't ask—'

'You didn't stop him.'

'I couldn't! I didn't want to make a scene!'

'Then don't make one now.'

'Tristan . . .'

But his mouth stopped her protest, and his hands held her when she tried to escape his hard embrace. His kiss was savage, unloving, and uncaring of the hurt he inflicted, and when he took her wrists in one hand to run the other over the soft contours of her body, it was not a caress but an insult.

She resisted him furiously, every nerve stretched to breaking point, every muscle straining uselessly against his assault, even when she knew it was hopeless fighting him, that all she could do was endure the punishment until he chose to stop.

At first outrage swamped every other emotion, but as she felt the strength in him, and the violence of his anger, she began to be frightened. This was no longer the man who had exercised such restraint when he had kissed her, who had been barely affected by kisses which left her weak and breathless. This was a stranger, a man thoroughly aroused to a raging desire. He was holding her so closely she couldn't help but be aware of it. This was a man who didn't care that she was too frightened to respond to him and not nearly strong enough to fight him. He was in his own private whirlpool, and he was pulling her down into it with him. . . .

She felt the blackness closing in about them, felt her resistance collapse in mindless fear, and then his mouth left hers and his arms slackened. She dragged one hand free and lashed out, felt her hand connect stingingly with his hard jaw, and then hot tears stung her eyes and she groped for the door handle, flung it open and left it that way as she fled blindly up the steps.

Sharon had left the door on the latch, and she locked it behind her with shaking fingers, one hand pressed to her mouth to stifle her gasping sobs, in case Sharon should hear.

She dropped her wrap on the floor and made for the bathroom, and as she reached the door it opened, and Sharon stood there, her blue eyes red-rimmed, her cheeks blotched with crying, her pretty mouth drooping.

'Oh, no!' she said, her mouth curling into a wry, wavering grin. 'You, too?'

Larissa couldn't manage to match the grin. Her eyes wide and tear-filled, she looked back at her friend and nodded wordlessly.

'Join the club,' Sharon invited, and held out her arms. 'What a perfectly ghastly evening!'

'Oh, Sharon!' Larissa mustered a watery giggle, on the edge of hysteria.

They clung together for comfort, and a little later Sharon said, 'Well, that's the end of a beautiful friendship, as far as Dennis is concerned.'

'Oh, Sharon, I'm sorry!' Larissa said, her voice husky with crying.

'Oh, what the heck, we were pretty well washed up, anyway. Tonight just hurried it along a bit, I guess. You didn't have a fight with Tristan about us, did you?'

Larissa shook her head. Her throat tightened, and

she looked away from the worried sympathy in her friend's eyes. 'I was disappointed that the evening wasn't a success,' she said evasively. 'I wanted you to like Tristan.'

'Yes, I know.' Sharon yawned. 'Well, nobody's perfect. If *you* like him, and you're sure you want him, I'll do my best to tolerate the man, which is about what he'll do for me, I reckon. You okay, now?'

Larissa nodded. Sharon wanted to go to bed, and she supposed she had better go, too. But she knew she wouldn't sleep. The trouble was, she wasn't at all sure that she did want Tristan. She wasn't even sure if she liked him. The only thing she was sure of, with a deep, sickening knowledge, was that she was afraid of him.

Chapter Six

The following day was Sunday, and if they didn't attend church, the two girls usually slept late. But Larissa heard Sharon in the kitchen quite early and went to join her.

'I'm going to visit my family,' Sharon told her. 'If I know Dennis, he'll be round here full of remorse and promises as soon as his hangover wears off, and I just don't feel like coping with him this morning.'

Larissa smiled sympathetically, then was jarred by the sudden thought that possibly Tristan might try to see her today, too. Her stomach knotted with fear, and she said breathlessly, 'Can I come?'

'Yes, of course. They'll be delighted.'

Larissa had visited Sharon's home on several previous occasions but not since her engagement. The Thompsons lived near Masterton, on the farm where Sharon had spent her childhood, and their children's friends were always welcome in the sturdy kauri and corrugated iron farmhouse set in rolling green paddocks.

As the bus took them along the wide motorway skirting the harbour Larissa looked at the waves hurling themselves against the brown rocks just below, and the misty rain obscuring the hills that ran down to the water at the other side of the harbour, and felt her own mood at one with the elements, turbulent and clouded. The Hutt Valley, with its industrial sprawl, did nothing to lift her spirits. But once they had passed through the satellite city of Upper Hutt and begun to climb the Rimutaka Range, which cut off the capital from the farming district of the Wairarapa, the sun was breaking bravely through ragged clouds, and even though the wind buffeted the bus when they reached the summit at eighteen hundred and twenty feet, Larissa breathed more freely during the descent to the other side of the mountains.

The air on the farm was crisp and clear, and in the afternoon Larissa took a long walk over the neatly fenced paddocks with Sharon and her younger sister, the only one of the four children who still lived at home. Sharon and Marjorie chatted, and Larissa walked thoughtfully, her mind busy.

On their return to the house, Mrs. Thompson remarked that Larissa looked pale, and Sharon's father teased her about her lack of appetite when they had an early tea. Larissa smiled wanly and assured them that she was quite all right. And she was, she told herself. She was calm, sure of herself for the first time in weeks, but the thought of what she intended to do sent her stomach into a flurry of sensations, none of them pleasant.

Sharon's father was out working some sheep when it came time for Mrs. Thompson to take the two girls to the bus stop in the family car. Sharon ran across to say good-bye to him, slipped as she was clambering over a wooden gate, and fell heavily on her arm.

When they picked her up, she yelped with pain and promptly fainted. The arm, the doctor confirmed when she had been rushed into town for treatment, was certainly broken. He put it in plaster and prescribed painkillers, and Sharon returned home to be put to bed and fussed over by her family.

The bus, of course, had gone long ago, but Larissa telephoned and found there would be another much later, not reaching the city until midnight. In spite of the Thompsons' urging to stay, and her own cowardly desire to accept, she insisted on going. If she put off what she was going to do, she might find herself lacking the courage to do it at all.

The bus had few empty seats, and at first she didn't notice the young man who sat himself beside her, a rucksack wedged between his booted feet.

When she sensed that he kept casting surreptitious glances at her, she didn't heed them. She was not unused to receiving second and third looks from men.

But when the bus took a sharp turn and her jacket slid from the luggage rack above them, they both reached to catch it, and she looked at his face and saw the eager question in his eyes, the tentative smile on his face, and felt recognition stirring.

He half stood to push her jacket back into the rack, then returned his eyes to her face, and Larissa stared, returning the doubtful smile.

'Larry?' he said, still not sure. And Larissa's smile burst forth dazzlingly.

'Jeffrey!' she said, certain now, and put out one hand and then the other, to be taken in his.

He squeezed her fingers, his own face lit with a delighted grin. 'I thought it was you,' he said. 'But if it wasn't, I might have got my face slapped.'

'You could have just said—'

'What? "Haven't we met before?" It's been done to death. And if you looked down your nose and said, *no,* I'd have felt a proper fool.'

'But you know my name!'

'Yes, but if I had made a mistake, you'd still think

I was trying to pick you up—if you'd been someone else. You know me, the shy type.'

Larissa laughed. 'Well, I'm not someone else. I'm me. And how marvellous to see you again! It's fantastic!'

'Well, it's a small country. You look terrific; I never realised when we were kids, but you're not bad-looking, you know that?'

'Well, don't sound so surprised!' she laughed at him. 'I missed you,' she told him.

'I missed you too, at first. But I was never much good at letters, and somehow . . .'

'I know,' she said swiftly. 'Neither was I, at that age. How's your mother?'

'Good. She married again, you know. Got a whole new family. I've got two little brothers and a sister, now. They live up north, the Bay of Islands.'

'I guess you'd forgotten about me.'

'Nope. I told my new sister about you. She's four, a real cutie. I'll miss them.'

'You don't live with them?'

'Off and on. But I've just got a job on the Cook Strait ferry run. That's why I'm on my way to Wellington.'

She led him on to tell her about his mother's family, all about his life since they had parted, their tenuous brother-and-sister relationship snapped when he had been removed from their foster home while Larissa stayed on. They digressed to childhood memories, laughing over remembered escapades and exchanging what scraps of information they could about the other children they had both known.

The journey passed swiftly, and when they emerged into the chill of the bus terminal, they were still talking, still trying to catch up on the years.

'Where are you staying?' Larissa asked.

'Don't know yet. I'll find a place. Too late for a hostel, I guess, but there must be some hotel that I could afford for one night. Give me your address, Larry. Do you have a phone? I'll contact you.'

'Why don't you come home with me?' she said impulsively. 'You can have Sharon's bed for the night. She won't mind.'

He looked doubtful. 'Are you sure?'

'Of course I'm sure, dope! There's a perfectly good bed going to waste. You won't even have to sleep on the sofa.'

A gust of wind thrust its way between them, making dropped papers on the pavement stir into life, whipping Larissa's hair across her eyes, and causing them both to shiver in its sudden icy touch.

'I don't know . . .' Jeffrey said.

For the past hour or so she had scarcely remembered the future, had buried the thought of it in reminiscing about the past. Suddenly the prospect of returning to the flat alone was chilling, like the wind.

'Do come, Jeff,' she pleaded. 'I want you to.'

'Well, okay.' He shrugged. 'I must admit, I don't fancy my chances at this hour of the night in a strange city.'

'No,' she said solemnly. 'I think I'd better protect you.'

'Huh!' He tweaked a handful of her hair in a well-remembered gesture, and they were two children again, laughing and making faces at each other, running madly to secure a taxi before it left the terminal empty, collapsing together onto the backseat, panting and grinning with juvenile triumph as they subsided on the smooth leather, and pooling the contents of pocket and purse at the end of the journey to pay their fare.

He unrolled his sleeping bag on top of Sharon's bed, refusing to let her change the sheets for him, and then Larissa made some coffee, and they sat in the living room and sipped it, talking quietly.

He reached over and touched the solitaire diamond on her finger. 'Hey!' He grinned. 'What's this? You didn't tell me you were engaged.'

Larissa put down her cup, the smile dying from her face. 'I was,' she said. 'I'm going to break it off. Tomorrow. I mean, today.'

Jeffrey looked slightly stunned, his grey eyes suddenly as serious as hers. 'Why?'

'Because,' she said, 'he scares me.'

Jeffrey frowned. 'Scares you? Is he violent?'

'Not the way you mean,' she said hastily. 'At least, he never has been. . . .'

'What's he done?' Jeffrey said, suddenly looking aggressive. 'Has he threatened you?'

She shook her head. 'Not . . . exactly. I can't explain,' she said, shivering slightly. 'I work for him. I'll have to go in tomorrow, and—give him this.' She took the ring from her finger and placed it on the low table in front of them. 'I'll have to find another job, too, I suppose.'

'Will he sack you?'

'I couldn't keep working there.'

Jeffrey grimaced. 'I suppose it would be awkward,' he acknowledged. 'If there's anything I can do to help . . . ?'

She shook her head, then gave a nervous little laugh. 'Unless you'd like to hold my hand while I tell him.'

He looked at her quickly, and she said, 'No, I don't mean it. But I'm dreading it. I hope I don't lose my nerve when it comes to the point.'

Her voice shook and Jeffrey frowned again. 'You *are* scared,' he said. 'Why did you get engaged to him in the first place?'

'Oh, he's very . . . attractive,' she said wryly. 'In a steely sort of way. And then I—oh, I don't know,' she added vaguely. 'I suppose he sort of—well, he tends to get what he wants. He's a bit . . . overpowering.'

'There are other people in this office, aren't there?' Jeffrey asked abruptly.

'Oh, yes. Lots.'

'Well if he gets too *overpowering* tomorrow, scream.'

Larissa couldn't imagine that Tristan would do anything to make her scream tomorrow. He might make her weep, or shake with fear, but he wouldn't do anything that would bring other people rushing in to see what was happening.

The knowledge steadied her a little, and she managed a small grin as she said, 'Yes, I will. But I won't need to. He won't go berserk. He's very—controlled.'

'Well, then . . .' Jeffrey looked relieved, thinking she had made a mountain out of a molehill. Perhaps she had; it was difficult to express the conviction she felt that behind Tristan's control lurked something terribly dangerous, something she didn't want to bring out in the open.

'I'm just not sure he'll take no for an answer,' she muttered.

Surprisingly, she slept soundly, and woke later than usual. Jeffrey was still curled up in his sleeping bag, dead to the world, and she shook him awake and flew into the bathroom, telling him he could have his turn in ten minutes.

She was under the shower when the telephone shrilled half a dozen times or more, and by the time she had quickly rubbed herself down with a towel and flung on a robe, it had stopped. She emerged to find Jeffrey standing by the phone looking rather sheepish.

'Who was it?' she asked.

'I didn't answer it. I wasn't sure . . . well, would your friends be shocked if a man answered your phone before breakfast?'

'They'd be a bit surprised, I suppose,' she admitted. Then she grinned, 'But you're not a man, anyway, you're my—' She stopped. 'Well, almost a brother.'

He was wearing hastily-pulled-on jeans and no shirt, and his hair was tousled. His tanned chest was hairless, and except for the stubble of beard on his cheeks and chin, he looked very much like the little boy she used to see every morning, sleepy-eyed and rough-haired.

'The bathroom's all yours,' she said. 'I'll make some breakfast.'

She and Sharon usually had a bowl of cereal and a piece of toast each, but Jeffrey rated something a bit more substantial. She set the table swiftly for two, and took bacon and eggs from the refrigerator and fried them. Jeffrey hadn't yet used the bathroom. He rolled up his sleeping bag, took some clothes and toilet gear from his pack, and disappeared, then came into the kitchen with an electric shaver and said, 'My razor's not working. It must have got damaged in my pack. Do you have something I can use?'

'Would a safety razor do?'

'Better than nothing,' he said. 'I'd hate to turn up for the new job looking like something the cat dragged in.'

She found one for him, but now the bacon and eggs were ready, so they had breakfast before he went off to shower and shave.

Larissa was still finishing her coffee when the door bell rang, a long impatient peal, and when she went to open the door her eyes were wide with puzzled apprehension.

She had barely moved back the catch when Tristan pushed at the panels with the flat of his hand and walked in. 'Why don't you answer your phone?' he asked tersely. 'Or is it out of order?'

'I was in the shower,' she said.

'So where's Sharon?'

'Staying with her parents. She had—'

'Good. I want to talk to you alone.'

He swung the door shut behind them and took her arm, and she said, walking beside him, 'I want to talk to you, too, Tristan. But . . .'

They were standing in the middle of the living room when the bathroom door opened and Jeffrey came out, zipping up his jeans, a towel flung about his bare shoulders, calling, "Hey, Larry, have you got a comb I could—'

He stopped short in the doorway of the living room, looking at Tristan. And Tristan, after a swift jerk of his head at the unexpected voice, and a brief, disbelieving look at Jeffrey, swept a slow, comprehensive glance about the room, with the table in the corner near the kitchen holding the remains of breakfast for two, the man's jacket that Jeffrey had casually left on the sofa, and the open doors of the two bedrooms, Larissa's bed still tumbled as she had stepped out of it, and Sharon's looking unused since Jeffrey had carefully smoothed it after removing his sleeping bag and replacing it in the pack he had stowed behind the door.

Then his narrowed, dangerous glance returned to Jeffrey, and he said very softly, 'And who the hell are you?'

Larissa's mouth went dry with terror. Her brain scrabbled frantically for the right word to describe who Jeffrey was, but her memory jammed, refusing to supply the correct term. The silence stretched, and she stammered, 'He's my brother—sort of. I mean, when we were children—he's my foster-brother!' she managed at last, the word suddenly presenting itself, too late.

Tristan was looking at her now, his gaze making her shiver. 'Just remembered you told me you had no family, Larissa?' he asked, barely moving his lips.

'We met on the bus last night,' she said. 'I mean, met again.'

'What a coincidence!' Tristan murmured, his eyes like glittering, colourless ice chips. 'What bus? If it matters. I was trying to contact you all day yesterday —up until midnight.'

'I went to Masterton with Sharon and came back on the late bus. Jeffrey was on it, and he had nowhere to stay.' Belatedly, she said, 'Jeffrey this is Tristan Sharpe, my—my employer.' She should have said *fiancé*, but that seemed farcical when she was planning to break their engagement and Jeffrey knew it. And then she compounded the disaster, saying, 'This is Jeffrey—' She faltered there, remembering at first only the name of their foster-parents, then recalling his true name, but hesitating again, realising that he might have taken his mother's new married name.

Jeffrey's look would have been comical in other circumstances, combining apology, wry understanding, and dismay. 'Grayson,' he told her.

And Tristan said, 'This gets better and better. You can't even remember the name of the man you just spent the night with—if you ever knew it!'

'I *haven't* just—' Larissa began, but Jeffrey had come away from the door, his fists bunched, looking belligerent. 'What are you suggesting?' he demanded, cutting in on Larissa's protest.

Tristan cast another glance about the room, and raised his brows slightly. '*Didn't* you spend the night here?' he asked pointedly.

Jeffrey flushed and said, 'Yes. But you have no right to—'

'I have every right!' Tristan said cuttingly. 'I suppose Larissa forgot to mention that she's engaged to me?'

Jeffrey said, 'She did mention it, actually.' Then

added levelly, 'She also mentioned that she intends to break it off.'

Something came and went in Tristan's face, and Larissa winced inwardly with fear. Then he said with deadly intent, 'Really . . . ? Was that before, after —or during?'

Jeffrey started forward, his mouth tight and his fist swinging back, and Larissa lunged at him, clinging, screaming, *'No! Jeffrey, don't!'*

'Okay, okay,' he muttered reluctantly, and put his arm about Larissa's shoulders.

Tristan hadn't moved an inch. He was surveying them both with ironic interest, apparently indifferent, except that his eyes still held that frightening glitter. Quite calmly, he said, 'I think you'd have found she had changed her mind this morning—if I hadn't unfortunately intruded. You see, I have quite a lot of money.'

'Tristan!' Larissa said in a shocked whisper. 'You know I don't want your money!'

'It appears I know very little about you,' he said, and his gaze seemed to sear as it swept over her. 'You lying little tramp!'

Jeffrey's arm dropped from Larissa's shoulders, and he stepped forward, looking dangerous. 'That's enough!' he said forcefully. 'One more crack like that and I'll smash your face in!'

Tristan looked at him with contempt and said, 'Try.'

'No!' Larissa cried. 'Please, Jeffrey. I don't want anyone fighting over me.' She felt sick. If they came to blows it would be terrible; she knew it. Jeffrey was a healthy young animal, but Tristan was taller and, in spite of his elegant suit, supremely fit; what's more, she was sure that he would not hesitate to use methods that Jeffrey had never even heard of.

Jeffrey was watching Tristan with increasing dislike, and Tristan knew it and was goading him. She had her hand on Jeffrey's arm, over the bunched muscle. She could feel his tension, although he held back for her sake. But he couldn't help hurling words at the man who watched him with such amused indifference. 'I'm not surprised that Larry changed her mind about marrying you!' he grated.

The amusement increased, insultingly. 'You really think she did? Well, the question is academic now. I've never been interested in secondhand goods.'

Larissa gasped and tightened her hold on Jeffrey's bare arm. He put his hand over hers and held it strongly.

His eyes still on Tristan, he snarled, *'Shut up!* You're supposed to be in love with the girl, aren't you? And you come barging in, jumping to conclusions, calling her names. You haven't even given her a chance to explain!'

'Not true. I simply don't find her explanation very plausible.'

'You didn't bloody listen!' Jeffrey shouted. 'Give her a chance, will you?'

Something flared in the steely eyes. Scepticism? Hope? Then Tristan ostentatiously folded his arms, assuming an apparently attentive stance, and said, 'All right. I'm listening.'

Jeffrey was holding Larrisa's hand tightly, and she was grateful for the contact. He said harshly, 'You don't owe him a thing, Larry. But tell him, if you want to.'

Larissa looked at the pitiless man facing her, his mouth twisting into a sneer as he dropped his eyes momentarily to the hand clasped in Jeffrey's, his eyes accusing, already disbelieving. She could tell him exactly what had happened, and how, and perhaps he would believe her. Perhaps not. It all seemed pointless anyway. What would be the use? Whatever there had been between them was all over now.

She said flatly, 'No. I'm not making any excuses or

apologies.' She met Tristan's eyes, her own steady and hopeless. 'Jeffrey spent the night here, with me. Make what you like of it. I don't care. I'm not ashamed. Now, please go. I—won't be coming into work today; I'll be looking for another job.'

'Very wise, under the circumstances,' he said, colourlessly. He unfolded his arms and looking at Jeffrey said, 'You poor young fool. Frankly, you're welcome to her.'

He turned his back immediately, and Larissa tightened her fingers on Jeffrey's as she felt him tense again.

Tristan had gone before she realised that his ring was still lying on the table where she had left it the night before.

Jeffrey had to go, of course. With a new job at stake, he couldn't afford to be late. Larissa assured him that she was all right, and he kissed her pale cheek awkwardly and promised to phone her as soon as his first Strait voyage was completed.

Larissa suppressed a strong urge to weep, put through a call to Masterton to be assured that Sharon was feeling fine and would be back shortly, and then sat down with the morning paper opened at the *Situations Vacant* columns.

She had fixed two appointments for the afternoon and was writing a letter applying for a third job, after a lunch of cheese on toast and a cup of tea, when the telephone rang.

'Larissa?'

Tristan, sounding as impersonal and remote as she had ever heard him. She gripped the receiver with shaking fingers and said briefly, 'Yes.'

· 'I have your wage packet made up, and two weeks pay in lieu of notice.'

'I don't want them!'

'Don't be a fool,' he said calmly. 'This is business, nothing to do with our personal . . . affairs.' He paused. 'You'll need money while you're job hunting. I've written you a reference, too.'

'That's very kind,' she said sarcastically. 'What does it say, that I'm honest and trustworthy?'

He let the silence extend and then said, 'You can come and collect them any time.'

'No.' She tried to emulate his cold, businesslike manner. 'Please post them.'

Again there was a pause. Then he said in just the same manner, 'If you haven't called to pick them up by five tomorrow, I'll bring them round to you and deliver them personally.'

Her protest was cut off by the receiver clicking down in her ear.

She would have to collect them. She didn't want Tristan coming to the flat again, especially while she was alone. And after two interviews made awkward by the fact that she could produce no reference from her previous employer, she reluctantly made her way to the offices of T. J. Sharpe.

The woman at the reception desk smiled at her, looking slightly puzzled. Larissa felt embarrassed, wondering if the staff knew the engagement was off.

'Are you all right?' the woman asked uncertainly. Larissa knew she looked pale, washed out; that was the way she felt. But she said, 'Yes, I'm fine.'

'We wondered if you were sick—when you didn't come in.'

So they didn't know. 'No,' she said. 'My flatmate had a slight accident.' Let the woman think she had been looking after Sharon. Before any more questions could be asked, she said hastily, 'Has Mr. Sharpe left anything for me?'

Looking mystified, the receptionist said no, but he was in; why didn't she go and speak to him?

'Yes, I will.' Larissa smiled at her and went on. They would know soon enough, but she wouldn't be there then to endure the stares and the speculation.

Briefly she wondered how Tristan would stand it, and the answer was obvious. He wouldn't show any sign of embarrassment, of course, and anyone timorous enough to broach the subject would be instantly cut down with an icy glare.

Miss Collins said, 'Mr. Sharpe is expecting you.' She nodded towards the door and added, 'You can go in.'

She went in and shut the door, standing in front of it, and Tristan rose slowly from the chair behind the desk, staring at her.

Several seconds ticked by while they measured each other, like adversaries, and then he said, 'Please sit down, Larissa.'

'I'd rather not.' She walked slowly forward. 'If you would just give me my pay . . .' She opened the bag swinging from her shoulder and extracted an envelope. 'Your ring,' she said, placing it on the desk. 'I should have given it to you this morning. I'm sorry.'

He looked down at the white envelope with the small bulge made by the ring he had given her. 'This morning,' he repeated, and then his eyes lifted very suddenly, almost as though he meant to catch her unawares. 'I wonder if we weren't all a little—'

'I don't want to talk about it,' she said swiftly. 'Let's leave it alone. Please.'

For an instant she saw naked fury in his gaze, then he veiled it and slowly took a long manila envelope from the desk drawer and stood with it in his hand.

'I'd been phoning you all day Sunday, you know,' he said. 'I even went round to the flat once. When you hadn't arrived home by midnight, I wondered if . . . something had happened to you.'

'You were worried?' She raised her eyes, surprised.

'Yes, *darn you,* I was worried! By this morning I was more than worried!'

She recoiled from the cold anger in his voice, his eyes. 'I'm sorry.'

His mouth tightened as he looked at her, and then he said, 'And all the time, you were . . .'

She winced, looking away from the ugly accusation in his face.

'I would never have believed it,' he said, so quietly he might have been talking to himself.

'Until you saw the evidence,' she suggested, taunting a little, because she felt bitter.

'The evidence *was* there.'

'And you drew your own conclusions.'

'You didn't deny it,' he said, harshly. 'You admitted he spent the night with you—'

He broke off suddenly, and she looked up, seeing a queer light in his eyes that she didn't understand, but it made her breath lock in her throat with fright.

'I took it you were using a euphemism,' Tristan said, still in that strange, harsh voice. 'Was I wrong?'

She was ready to say, yes—*yes you were wrong*.

But she saw the look on his face, then; it was taut and angry, with the frightening glitter in his eyes that she remembered from Saturday night, when he had kissed and caressed her in that terrifyingly violent way. She felt the power of his attraction for her, and the depth of her own barely understood fear. And she knew there was one way to cut free of him, to end the confusion that he had aroused in her, the strange, feverish pull that he exerted over her feelings.

'No,' she said deliberately. 'You were not wrong, Tristan.'

'I see,' he said quietly. He didn't move, but something died in his face, the frightening light faded from his eyes, leaving them cold, without expression. 'It wasn't the first time, of course.'

She said, 'You don't have any right to information about my private life any more.'

115

His mouth tightened. 'No,' he admitted, tone-lessly. 'No, you're right.'

He handed over the envelope, and as she took it and put it into her bag, he pushed at the white envelope containing his ring. 'You might as well keep this,' he said. 'It fits you, and I've no use for it.'

'No, thank you.' Her clipped tones matched his. 'I don't want it.'

'That makes two of us,' he said, and he scooped up the envelope, crushed it in his hand and tossed it into the wastebasket at the side of the desk.

'Tristan!' she gasped, horrified, and made an involuntary movement toward the basket.

He dropped into his chair, lounging back, a nar-row, unpleasant smile on his face. 'Changed your mind, darling?' he said. 'If you want it, take it.'

His foot moved, the toe of his elegant shoe giving the basket a shove, so that it shifted forward a little and then tipped, the crumpled envelope among the other rubbish scattering on the carpet.

'Go on,' he urged. 'Pick it up. You could sell it for a few thousand.'

She was tempted to pick the thing up and throw it in his jeering face. With an effort she controlled her temper, gave him a glance of angry disdain, and turned on her heel. At that moment she hated him with all her being. It was a feeling she cherished, hoping it would get her through the difficult weeks and months ahead, because she couldn't forget him, and the only way she could bear to live with the memory of him was to nurture her hatred.

Chapter Seven

It had all been a long time ago, and life had moved on. On her return from overseas, Larissa had deliberately chosen to live in Auckland rather than go back to Wellington. She had refused to examine her own motives, not wanting to acknowledge even to herself that she felt safer more than six hundred kilometres away from Tristan Sharpe.

As she boarded the bus that would take her from Pakuranga into the city, she wondered if he was on his way back to Wellington yet; and when they crossed the bridge spanning the Panmure Basin with its anchored pleasure craft lazily riding the quiet water and pohutukawas dipping silver-green branches from the cliffs, she remembered with a faint pang that he had been going to take her yachting, one day, and that the day had never arrived, after all.

Grimly, she pushed the thought aside. That was going back to years ago, when regret and depression had warred with relief from tension and confusion. She was *not,* she told herself fiercely, going to slip back into that ghastly morass of emotions because of one brief chance meeting, devastating though it had been. No more reliving the past.

The resolution lasted until she reached the Stenserve agency's office. She smiled at the receptionist, who said, 'Mrs. Stevens wants you in her office. I think there's a job for you.'

Good, Larissa thought. She hoped the job would keep her busy all day, too busy to think, to indulge in futile remembrances. . . .

She tapped on the door and went in, her smile ready, but it slipped badly as she realised that Mrs. Stevens was not alone, that the man sitting in the black leather chair before the desk, turning to watch her entrance, was Tristan.

She went cold and clutched at the handle of the door, because for a brief moment she felt dizzy. Her eyes, wide with shock, met his, and she thought she saw the familiar mockery in the blue gaze he shafted at her.

Mrs. Stevens, apparently noticing nothing, said, 'Oh, there you are, Larissa! Good. Mr. Sharpe has been waiting for you.'

Larissa steadied herself and took two steps into the room. 'Why?' she asked baldly.

'Well, it seems he was impressed with you yesterday—and I believe you've worked for him before. He has asked for you again.'

Mrs. Stevens looked pleased, expecting Larissa to feel complimented.

'I thought Mr. Sharpe would be back in Wellington by now,' Larissa said.

Tristan spoke then. 'I'm setting up a branch in Auckland,' he said. 'I'll be here for a few weeks, attending to the preliminary details, and I want a temporary secretary.'

A few weeks! Dismayed, she began to stammer, 'But I don't think—'

'You're lucky to get Larissa, Mr. Sharpe.' Mrs. Stevens beamed as she interrupted. 'She's one of our best. I'm sure you'll be very happy with her.'

'So am I.' He turned to Larissa and said, 'I've a lot to get through today. Do you have a notebook with you? Perhaps we could leave now.'

She looked in despair at Mrs. Stevens, even thought of refusing the job point-blank, but she couldn't do that without a reason. And trying to give her reasons to the woman would be embarrassing. She didn't want to explain the personal relationship between herself and Tristan Sharpe, even in the briefest terms.

Reluctantly, she allowed him to take her arm lightly and went with him to the elevator.

He pressed the button, and she moved away from him and said stiffly, 'Is it true? That you need a temporary secretary?'

'Perfectly true.' He looked coldly bored. 'Why should I lie?'

'Why did you ask for me, particularly?' she asked, her eyes fixed challengingly on his face.

The lift jerked to a halt, and just as the doors were sliding apart, he said, 'Mrs. Stevens just told you that.'

There were people waiting to get in, and he steered her through them and out into the street. 'I have to look at some possible offices,' he said. 'I want you to make notes as we go. Advantages, disadvantages of each one. Anything I tell you to write down, and anything that strikes you as well. You'd know something about desirable layouts as far as they affect the secretarial staff.'

He seemed so strictly businesslike that she was deterred from accusing him outright of having a personal reason for requesting her services. It was as though last night had never been, and as they inspected the various premises available, she slipped back into the role of secretary to a demanding, incisive professional man who expected efficiency and was used to getting it.

When he asked her opinion she was at first reluctant to give it, but when he showed a slight impatience, his mouth tightening fractionally while his eyes raked her with chill annoyance, she reminded herself that she was here to do a job, and that giving her opinion was apparently part of it. She crisply reeled off a list of problems she saw in the offices they were looking at, and he listened in silence, then gave a nod and said, 'Yes, I thought that, too. We'll go on to the next one, shall we?'

By lunchtime, he had chosen his new offices, on the fourth floor of a new downtown building with plenty of floor space on which he could design his own layout, and large windows letting in plenty of natural light.

'Any comments?' he asked Larissa, and she lifted her shoulders and said, 'It seems ideal.'

'That's it, then.' He turned to the man who had let them in and said, 'I believe there's an apartment that's available in this building, too?'

'Up the top,' the man answered. 'Want to see it?'

It was empty but had a view of the harbour, efficient kitchen and bathroom arrangements, and a good layout. This time, Tristan didn't ask Larissa to give an opinion, but as they left the suite, he said, 'Would you like to choose the furnishings for me?'

'I'm a secretary, Mr. Sharpe, not an interior decorator,' she answered.

'I know that. But most women seem to enjoy any chance to play amateur decorator.'

'I'm sure you're used to engaging the very best experts for anything you want, Mr. Sharpe. I doubt if my efforts would satisfy you.'

The other man had gone ahead and was pressing

the lift button, his eyes on the floor indicator as he waited for the lift to arrive.

Very softly, Tristan said, 'A gifted amateur can often be as good as a professional. And you know I'd pay for your services—secretarial or otherwise.'

She clenched her teeth and stared woodenly ahead as the elevator doors opened and they walked in. She avoided looking at him until he was opening the door of his hired car, and he touched her arm and said, 'What's the matter?'

She gave him a look of sheer dislike and got in without answering.

Tristan closed the door behind her and walked round to slide into the driver's seat. They were parked near the top of a multistory parking garage, on an open deck, looking down on the harbour and many of the older, intervening office blocks and shops. He turned to look at her and said, 'I asked you a question.'

Her mouth tightened, but she didn't look at him. His hand came under her chin, forcing her to face him, and she lifted a closed fist to knock it aside, her eyes blazing.

'Don't *touch* me!' she said. 'And don't make any more of your snide, clever remarks at my expense, either!'

'I don't know what you're talking about,' he said in clipped tones.

'You know *perfectly well* what I'm talking about! I had enough of your beastly innuendos and insulting offers last night. Well, in future you can pay someone *else* for whatever services you require, Mr. Sharpe—secretarial or otherwise! I'm not available for any of them! Mrs. Stevens will find you another secretary, but I should warn you that if you offer to buy any of those other *services* from her, you'll be politely shown the door. Stenserve is not running a call-girl business.' She paused for breath, and said shakily, 'I think I would rather make my own way back, thank you. I'll tell Mrs. Stevens to expect you later.'

She tried to open the door, but Tristan leaned across and prevented her, his arm almost touching her, his hand firmly on the latch.

'Just a minute,' he said. 'The fact is, I didn't mean what you obviously think I did.' His tone was faintly amused. 'I honestly meant no more than what I said—the subject under discussion was interior decorating, nothing else.'

His eyes were steady and hard, and she drew a quick, deep breath, flushing deeply. At last she said, with difficulty, 'I'm sorry. But last night—'

'Ah, last night,' he said, sitting back in his seat. 'That's a different story. I thought you knew that I seldom mix business with—pleasure.'

He started the car and began to pull out of the parking space, his hand resting on the seat behind her as he backed out, looking through the rear window.

His eyes met hers briefly before he turned and changed the gears, his expression unreadable, and then he said, 'Do up your safety belt,' and headed the car down the ramp towards the exit.

Larissa didn't ask who the apartment was for; she guessed that a branch manager would be installed in it eventually, but meantime it was quickly furnished, and while the offices below were being prepared for occupation, Tristan and she often worked on the upper floor. A long table served as a desk for her, and Tristan did paperwork sitting on the dark blue sofa facing the view of the Waitemata and the island volcano, Rangitoto, from the lounge window. The room had been furnished in shades of blue, light walls and dark upholstery, with a grey-blue wall-to-wall carpet and a couple of large white sheepskin rugs. A long glass-topped coffee table in front of the sofa usually held a selection of neatly ordered papers, and with the typewriter sharing the dining table with a small metal filing cabinet, the atmosphere was that of a fairly luxurious office rather than anyone's home, although Larissa knew that Tristan had moved in and was sleeping in the bedroom, which she had not seen since it was furnished. She supposed it was cheaper and more convenient than putting up at a hotel.

There was no hint of intimacy in their relationship. Tristan was strictly her employer, and she was careful never to let a personal note intrude. Occasionally she found him regarding her with a withdrawn, speculative glance, which she returned with a look of cool enquiry until he turned back to the work in his hand, or made some business-related comment.

Apparently he still made a practice of interviewing prospective employees personally. He had advertised for staff, and a procession of hopefuls took up most of the second week. Larissa was kept busy typing formal letters of acceptance or rejection.

In the third week, Larissa could see her job coming to a close. There were only a few loose ends left; the new branch was virtually ready to go into business.

On Wednesday Tristan handed her a letter of application to be answered and said, 'I can't use this man. Tell him the position is filled. By the way, an old friend has asked me to go sailing with him and his wife this weekend. I'm supposed to bring someone to make a foursome. Would you like to come?'

She looked up at him in swift surprise, and when she didn't answer, he said, 'Well?'

'Is this business or pleasure?' she asked cautiously.

'Call it a bonus if you like,' he answered. 'You've been an exceptionally good secretary and I'd like to show my appreciation. But we won't be working over the weekend.'

'A whole weekend on board?'

'Yes. You'll enjoy it. We sail on Friday evening.'

She fingered the letter he had handed to her and said carefully, 'What sort of foursome do your friends have in mind?'

'They're not swingers, if that's what you're thinking. They're good company, but fairly conventional in their morals. Does it sound too dull to interest you?'

'It doesn't sound dull at all. But if you're going to make cracks like that . . .'

'All right,' he said, and suddenly his hand went over hers on the table, holding it firmly. 'No cracks. I promise. Will you come?'

She moved her fingers experimentally, and he lifted his hand immediately. 'The job will finish this week, won't it?' she asked abruptly.

'Yes. Sorry?'

'It's been . . . interesting.'

'I thought this weekend would be a good way to round things off. We've both worked hard, and a leisurely cruise would be a pleasant way to unwind.'

Larissa looked out at the haze lying over the city and the intermittent glitter of the sun on water glimpsed between the buildings. The weather was still very hot; Auckland's high humidity intensified the effect of the sun, so that everyone felt enervated and sticky. Out on the Gulf there would be cool sea breezes. The thought was tempting.

'No strings?' she asked, looking up at him, and he smiled faintly and said, 'No strings.'

'Then . . . thank you. I'd like to come.'

When he was sitting on the sofa again, his fair head bent over the table as he made some swiftly scribbled notes, she watched him covertly. The last few weeks had been so different from the night when he had taken her home and kissed her, insulted and threatened her, that it all seemed like an unlikely nightmare now. She had enjoyed working with him, enjoyed watching him in action again, and trying to keep abreast of him, trying always to be prepared for the latest move, whether it was finding a document, taking a letter, or making a note of something he wanted to record or remember. They worked well together; they always had.

She realised that she was going to hate it when he went back to Wellington. That was why she had accepted his invitation. She tried to ignore the knowledge that she was going to miss him, that she wanted to spend the weekend with him because she dreaded the thought of not seeing him again.

She couldn't help speculating on why he had asked her. Simply a bonus for a job well done, as he had said? Or perhaps it was convenient to ask her, since his friends expected him to bring along a girl, and he couldn't know many in Auckland. Or—and it was a possibility she must face—if he had meant what he said about still wanting her, but not enough to offer her marriage, was this one of the calculated, patient manoeuvres at which he was such an expert in business, and which he was not above using in his private life?

She didn't know what went on inside that sleek head, behind those enigmatic eyes. She might be able to guess at his moods and anticipate his wants in the limited area of his business life, but his deeper feelings, his motives, the emotions that made him tick, were as much a mystery to her as ever.

When she met Brian and Gemma Forbes, she was immediately reassured. Brian was tall and bulky, with thick, curling black hair and the smile of a sometimes benevolent buccaneer. His handshake was bone breaking but his eyes were friendly, and his slow, 'Welcome aboard, Larissa,' was sincerely meant.

His wife was small and inclined to plumpness, bubbly red curls erupting over her head, tossed into her eyes by the wind as they made their way out of the harbour heading for the Hauraki Gulf, and blue eyes dancing with excitement. The sails unfurled with a crack that startled Larissa as she held on to the stern rail with Tristan's arm curved near, his hand on the rail close to hers, his shoulder behind her own, but not touching.

He went forward to help Brian as a ship steamed into the harbour, its wash tossing the yacht a little, and Larissa watched as he secured ropes and ducked under the boom when it swung a little towards his head. The breeze lifted his hair and blew it across his forehead, and he pushed it back impatiently with long fingers. He was wearing jeans and a short-sleeved cotton knit shirt, with a pair of sneakers on his feet that had definitely seen better days. She had never seen him look so casual or so carefree. The grin that he slanted to his friend as they worked the boat was entirely different from the narrow, cynical smile she was used to. His tan was not deep, but golden, and the fading sun burnished his hair with light, making it pale gold, too. He looked lean and handsome, and younger than when she had first met him five years ago.

Other craft swayed and slid past them, their crews waving and occasionally shouting a greeting, but as they sailed farther out to sea these became fewer, and soon the city was a smudge of blue behind them, prickled with early-evening lights. The spangled arch of the Harbour Bridge hung over an inky sea.

They passed Rangitoto, its volcanic cone rising mysteriously against the twilight sky, and some time later they dropped anchor in a sheltered bay and had a meal of cold meat and salad, sitting on cushions on the gently moving deck, while a morepork called in melancholy fashion from the dark, bush-laden shore.

They sipped cool drinks and talked into the night, and Larissa discovered that Tristan had been right when he said that his friends were good company. They were intelligent and well read, and their opinions were worth listening to. And Brian had a quiet sense of humour that his wife played up to with a more pungent wit of her own. Larissa found herself joining in eagerly, laughing and amicably arguing a point of view, stimulated by Brian's sceptical questioning and Gemma's quickness at picking up a point or finding a flaw in someone's logic.

Tristan seemed to hold aloof, watching them all and slipping in an occasional comment that would start them on a new track or crystallise the essence of the discussion, and after a time, when they were exchanging views on one of the latest best-selling novels, recently filmed, Larissa turned to him and asked, 'Have you read the book?'

'Yes,' he said.

'Well, what do you think?'

He looked at her thoughtfully, and she knew he was aware that he was being challenged. Then he told them, his opinion as incisive and penetrating as any reviewer's would have been. From then on he took a full part in the discussion, even making them laugh once or twice with his dryly caustic comments on certain authors and their books.

'I didn't know you were such a reader,' Larissa exclaimed at one point. 'I thought you were too busy for books.'

'I might have been, once.' he admitted. 'I've only recently come to reading fiction, as a matter of fact. *You* know more about it than I do.'

'How do you know?'

'You've always been a reader, haven't you? I remember that you used to get very enthusiastic if you liked a book. You forced me to read one, once.'

'Forced?' Gemma exclaimed. 'I don't believe it.'

'You needn't,' Larissa said promptly. 'It isn't true.'

'Well, let's say you pressed it on me with such eagerness that I felt obliged to read it.'

She remembered, now. It had been the novelized autobiography of a young girl's return from the borders of madness; she had read it during the brief period of their engagement and was so impressed by it that she had wanted to share it with him. But she had never found out what he thought of it, because it was at that time that their engagement came to its abrupt, disastrous end.

She didn't know how much the Forbeses knew about that, whether they were aware that Tristan had once asked her to marry him. She felt a little awkward suddenly, and the silence stretched uncomfortably, until Gemma said, 'Well, it's late, and I'm going to bed.'

'So will I,' Larissa said quickly. They both went down, leaving the men alone. There were two cabins and Gemma and Larissa were sharing one. Larissa was grateful that the arrangement seemed to be taken for granted. She didn't know exactly how Tristan had described their relationship, but evidently Gemma and Brian realised that it was not an intimate one. She thought he had probably simply said she was his temporary secretary and that he had brought her along to show his appreciation of her work.

They spent Saturday sailing lazily along close to the coastline, and the men fished without success while Larissa and Gemma sunbathed. Later in the day they all swam in the bracing depths of the sea and then sailed to a safe anchorage for the night.

Larissa was allowed a turn at the tiller with Tristan standing behind her, his hand lightly on her waist as he showed her what to do. When the wind changed, and she panicked a little and lurched sideways, his hand shifted and slipped beneath the light T-shirt she wore with her shorts. He righted them again and steadied both her and the tiller, but his hand stayed warm and firm on her skin, not moving, just *there*. She felt little waves of pleasure emanating from his touch, and her breath quickened. He was holding her fractionally closer now, perhaps to prevent a repetition of the incident, and she could feel the hardness of him at her back, and the soft, steady beating of his heart.

The water slapped the sides of the boat, and sea birds careened gracefully over their heads, calling distantly. A dolphin arched out of the blue ripples ahead and then disappeared, and Larissa's hair, which she had tied at her nape with a ribbon, suddenly came loose and whipped back in the wind.

'Oh!' she exclaimed, half turning, only then realising that Tristan was holding the ribbon in his hand.

'Watch the tiller,' he said sternly, and put her hands back on it, but now his hand was moving disturbingly on her midriff, the fingers delicately tracing her rib cage, his thumb roving until it found the soft curve of her breast.

Larissa pulled away sharply. 'I've had enough,' she said, 'You can steer.'

She slipped out of his hold, and he didn't try to detain her, but she knew his eyes followed her as she went forward to join Brian and Gemma, standing hand in hand in the bow.

They anchored that evening in the lee of one of the scattered islands, and bedtime came earlier, because they were all pleasantly, healthily tired.

The next morning they breakfasted ,late, and Gemma and Brian decided to explore the island, tramping off together into the thick scrub of manuka and bracken and disappearing into the taller bush farther inland, where golden akeake and glossy taupata merged with tall kohekohe and lancewood and a tangle of other native trees.

Larissa might have elected to go with them if she had not received an impression that the two of them had a desire to be alone for a while. She had seen them touching hands more than once, and she knew there was precious little opportunity for privacy on board the yacht.

She and Tristan swam the short distance to the narrow shore. Tristan lay back on an outcrop of smooth white rock and closed his eyes against the sun's glare while Larissa wandered along the shoreline exploring rock pools and then swam briefly again, floating lazily in the clear water, admiring the clean lines of the yacht and the curve of the shore lapped by the gentle, insistent sea. Tiny white manuka blossoms drifted by her.

She had pinned her hair up for swimming, but wet strands clung to her shoulders as she came out, her feet sinking a little in the hot sand, fragments of pipi and mussel and paua shells scratching her toes.

She walked to the flat rock projection where Tristan lay, apparently dozing. His body was smooth except for a light glinting fuzz of fair hair on his arms and legs, the dark swim shorts he wore emphasising the light tan on his torso. He wouldn't tan deeply, she supposed; his skin would be naturally fair, with his light hair and eyes, but the slight golden tint he had acquired was very attractive.

She edged closer, her feet noiseless on the soft sand, her body cool in a brief white bikini still wet from her swim, the droplets of water sliding down her arms and legs and dripping from her damp hair.

She was close enough to see Tristan's face, relaxed and tranquil, when she realised that a glint of blue was showing beneath the lowered eyelids, and that he was watching her.

She stopped short, only a yard or so from him, her nerves quivering.

Tristan opened his eyes properly, staring back into her startled face. 'Come on,' he said. 'Are you going to stand there all day?'

'I thought you were asleep.'

'What were you going to do? Wake me with a kiss?'

'Hardly,' she said dryly. 'I might have been tempted to pour some seawater over you.'

A faint grin etched his mouth, the sort of lazy, pleasant grin that she had seen him give to Brian and Gemma. 'Do,' he invited. 'If you're prepared for a reprisal.'

'Are you daring me?'

He got up suddenly, taking her by surprise, and leapt lightly down off the rock onto the sand. Larissa stepped backwards, but he had caught her bare waist in his hands, pulling her near even as she tried to lean away from him, her fingers closing over his arms to keep the distance between them.

'What if I am?' he asked her calmly.

'I don't take dares,' she said huskily. 'It's very— juvenile.'

'Mmm,' he said consideringly. 'And you're very adult, aren't you, Larissa?'

'I'm twenty-four.'

'Yes, I know. I wonder how much you've learned in five years. Have you graduated from the boys to the men?'

Larissa stiffened, and the hands holding her waist tightened. Larissa pushed hard at his arms, but he only shifted his grip, bringing her closely against him, his arms inescapable. 'How long did Jeffrey satisfy you?' he murmured.

'Stop it!' She lashed at him with her fist, but it

thudded harmlessly against his shoulder, and he laughed and said, 'Let's find out if practice really does make perfect.'

She tried to evade his seeking mouth, but it found hers anyway, hard, angry, yet insidiously sensual. She kept her lips firmly closed until he lifted a hand to her face, his thumb and fingers exerting pressure until her mouth parted involuntarily, and even as she moaned a protest he deepened the kiss inexorably and the cruel pressure became a soft, stroking caress, brushing over her throat and shoulder and down to the tiny bikini top to find her breast.

She shuddered at the touch, and his other hand slid lower, holding her tightly as he deliberately moved against her, a slow, insistent motion so that she could feel the force of his desire.

Shocked, she tried to pull away from him, but the suddenness of her withdrawal unbalanced them both, and she fell against the gritty sand with him on top of her.

He laughed softly, his legs entwined in hers, his warm thigh moving against the soft inner skin of hers. 'In such a hurry, darling?' he taunted, his hands holding her upper arms as she tried, panting, to push him off.

'Let me go! *Let me go or I'll—*'

'What will you do?' His grin was no longer easy and friendly; it was wolfish.

She felt the muscles of her stomach tauten, felt the heat of his body and the stirring of her own involuntary desire for him. He lowered his head and brushed his lips quite gently over her throat, licking at the saltwater between her breasts and murmuring, 'You taste of the sea.'

Sudden heat shot through her, and in desperation she lifted her knee quickly and hard, and he gave a sharp, hoarse cry and doubled up as she pushed at him and rolled away.

She crouched, watching him in fascinated horror, feeling sick, her eyes anxious.

He was pale when he straightened and looked at her, his eyes dangerous. When he moved she shot to her feet and sped into the water, making for the yacht. When she climbed aboard he was right behind her, his hand on her arm, spinning her to face him.

He had got back his colour, but his eyes were glittery and his mouth was set grimly. 'You little fool,' he said. 'Don't you know you should never do that to a man when there's no place to run to?'

'I'll scream,' she warned huskily.

'Will you? Brian and Gemma have been gone at least half an hour. It'll take them that long to get back. And there's no one else within miles.'

She raised her hand and swung it towards his face, and he moved quickly, evading the blow and then swinging her into his arms. She thought of the deserted cabins below and screamed, harsh and shrill, and pummelled at his shoulders and his hard, determined jaw.

It didn't last long. He took one long stride and then simply dropped her over the side.

The water closed over her head while she was still realising with stupefaction that he wasn't going to take her below and attack her after all. When she surfaced, she looked up at the deck, but he had disappeared. The shore was deserted, and she made for that, because she didn't want to be alone with Tristan, and she had a hunch he had had enough of her, too, for today.

She climbed over the rocks to a shady, secluded spot just out of sight of the yacht and sat down, her hands holding her lowered head. Of course Tristan wouldn't have raped her, either on the beach or aboard the yacht. He wasn't an undisciplined brute; he was a very civilised man, with more control over his instincts than most. Her fear had been born out of her own feelings, not his. She had been afraid that he would guess at how much he had aroused her, afraid of self-betrayal. Because he had only been conducting one of his cold-blooded experiments, seeing how deeply he could make her respond, even though he made no secret of his contempt for her. And it was too humiliating to let him know how readily he could do it.

She stayed where she was until she heard voices. Then she strolled around the rocks and accompanied Gemma and Brian back to the boat. They had lunch and then set sail for home, and Larissa was quite successful at disguising the fact that she was avoiding any direct contact or conversation with Tristan.

He looked just as usual, controlled, aloof, with an occasional absent smile for Gemma or Brian, his glance sliding over Larissa coolly, without appearing to notice her.

But when they were back in the boat harbour, and Gemma and Brian had gone below to get some of their things, she went over to where Tristan was leaning on the rail, looking at the city dreaming in the Sunday haze. 'Are you all right?' she asked in a low voice, not looking at him.

'I'm not crippled for life,' he answered, his voice dry. 'I was temporarily out of action—that was what you wanted, wasn't it?'

'I'm sorry if I hurt you—but you asked for it.'

'It was drastic. Do you often do that?'

'I've never done it in my life before. I've never needed to.'

If he suggested she had never wanted to, she thought, she would hit him. Hard.

Instead, he said, 'Were you frightened of me?'

She didn't answer, and he said, 'Dear me. I must be sadly lacking in finesse. I'll try to improve my technique.'

'You won't need to,' she said. 'I've told you I'm

not interested. And anyway, you'll be back in Wellington, surely, before the end of the week?'

'No, I won't. I'm taking over the Auckland operation myself. I thought you realised that.'

Her heart lurched, and she gripped the rail before her as though she would fall without its support.

'No!' she whispered. 'I didn't—I never thought—'

'Will you stay with me?'

She twisted to look at him, her eyes wide.

'I mean, will you stay on as my secretary?' he said. 'You know you're the best I've ever had, don't you?'

'Thank you,' she managed. 'But no.'

'I'll pay you very well.'

Suddenly angry again, she said, 'You can't buy me! Either as a secretary or a mistress. I just told you, no!'

'I nearly bought you once before,' he said, with deadly intent. 'For the price of a wedding ring.'

She would have hurled a bitter reply at him but Gemma came up on deck, and he turned away to help her with the bags she was carrying. She managed the trip to shore and the thanks to her hosts without looking Tristan's way again, but since they waited for her and Tristan to leave first, in his car, she had to suffer being taken home by him rather than create an embarrassing scene in front of his friends.

They had been driving for a few minutes when he said, 'Are you sure you wouldn't like to reconsider?'

"What do you think I am?' she exclaimed. 'Even if I was as mercenary and immoral as you've implied, do you think I'd be willing to put up with your snide accusations and beastly innuendos indefinitely? And who gave you the right to judge other people, anyway? Are you some kind of saint?'

'I'm not a liar,' he said. 'And I don't pretend to be something I'm not.'

'*I'm* not a liar, either!'

He didn't answer, and she closed her eyes despairingly, because of course she *had* lied to him. She had lied when she had let him think that Jeffrey was her lover, but he thought the true story was the lie. It was hopeless to try and make him believe her now.

'Was it so important,' she said, 'for your bride to be a virgin?'

'No. It was only important that she was honest with me.'

'If I was honest with you now,' she suggested tiredly, 'you wouldn't believe me.'

'Probably not,' he agreed coldly. 'So don't plead innocence at this late date.'

'It doesn't matter, anyway. After tonight, I never want to see you again.'

'You will,' he said softly.

'You can't force me—'

'I don't intend to. Your reaction this afternoon wasn't necessary, you know. I wouldn't have hurt you. Not physically.'

She shivered inwardly, because that was an admission. He might stop short of physical violence, but mental cruelty wasn't barred in his book. 'What do you *want* of me?' she whispered fiercely.

'I told you.'

Bitterly, she said, 'This is a big city. You can buy sex anywhere.'

'You know I don't want just sex.'

'No,' she said. 'That's too simple for you, isn't it? You have to have an additional fillip. Your pride took a blow when you thought I preferred someone else, and you've never recovered, have you? You're too cold-blooded to be interested in sex for itself. With you, it's either a clinical experiment or some perverted form of vengeance. Well, I had enough of being your laboratory specimen when we were engaged, and if it stung your ego to think you weren't the only man in my life, you'll just have to live with it. I'm not going to be your willing victim. I'm not going to sleep with you to restore your damaged self-image.'

The only sign that he had heard was a slight increase in their speed as he pressed down harder on the accelerator. But the silence stretched taut between them as he swung the car into her street and slowed, bringing it to a gliding halt outside the flats.

He had placed her bag on the rear seat, and as she turned to get it he put his hand on her arm and held her, taking her other arm, too, and holding her helpless, her fists clenched against his chest.

'Don't touch me,' she breathed unsteadily. 'I can't stand you touching me!'

'You didn't mind, on Saturday,' he said softly. 'I touched you then, and you didn't object.'

His breath stirred her hair as he spoke, his lips close to her temple. He bent closer, and his mouth brushed her skin. She jerked her head away.

'Your friends were there,' she said coldly. 'I didn't want to make a scene.'

'*And* you liked it,' he suggested, his lips trailing soft little kisses down the side of her neck as she strained away from him.

'No!' she gasped, 'I didn't! I . . .'

He pushed her back against the seat, his hands compelling, and she turned her head to look at him, to say, 'Don't!'

He released one of her arms, but it didn't help her, because it was trapped between their bodies, and he was bringing his hand along the slope of her shoulder to her nape, tipping her head to find her mouth with his.

She tried to close her mind to what he was doing, to the gentle, unbearably pleasurable feeling of his lips moving softly over hers, not cruel at all, but coaxing, first lightly, almost teasingly, and then firmer, questioning, demanding. A tide of sweetness flowed through her, and she clenched her fists hard and tried to push him away.

He raised his head then and looked at her wide, defiant eyes, and smiled a little. Against her lips, he said, 'You let me touch you like this. . . .' And he put his hand where it had been when he stood behind her at the tiller of the yacht, pushing under her blouse to find the warm smooth skin of her waist, and slid it upward until his thumb felt the softness it had discovered then. . . .

'No,' she moaned, but his thumb was still there, beginning a slow, sensual stroking movement over the now-tautened curve, and he whispered, 'Yes—oh, yes!' And his mouth searched hers again until she was almost sick with the longing to respond. His caress was driving her crazy with excitement and frustration and the frantic fear that if he didn't stop she was lost. And then he shifted his hand just fractionally, taking the soft weight of her breast in his palm, and that maddening stroking reached the small hardening nub at last . . . at last. . . .

Larissa moaned again, an inarticulate protest, but her treacherous body was betraying her, trembling with passion, her breasts taut and aching for his touch, her mouth submitting to his kisses, her back arching against his arm as she pressed herself closer to him.

All thought was suspended, deliciously, marvellously unimportant; only their entwined bodies existed in the whole universe, for an endless few minutes of time. Then Tristan lifted his mouth from hers and said, 'Let's go inside, darling.'

He leaned across her and opened her door, and reality entered with the cool night air. She began to realise with appalled shock what had happened in the last few minutes, and, even more, what he had every reason to believe was going to happen now.

'My bag,' she murmured. 'The key.'

He eased his hold on her, reached over to the backseat, and put the bag between them. Larissa fumbled, found the key, and took a firm grip on the overnight bag, then said, 'I think I've sufficiently thanked you for the weekend,' and shot out of the car, slamming the door behind her.

She was quick, but not quick enough, and by the time she had the door open he was right beside her, pushing the door wide so that they stepped into the flat together, his hand hard on her arm.

He snapped on the light switch, and she blinked in the glare, blinking again when she saw the icy rage in his eyes.

'Was that supposed to be some kind of joke?' he asked.

'Yes, actually. And the joke's on you. I already told you, no deal. You wouldn't take no for an answer, so I decided to string you along a bit. Now get out. If you don't, I have two burly neighbours who will be perfectly willing to throw you out. All I have to do is yell.'

His eyes were frightening, but his voice was flat and calm. 'You don't have to yell,' he said. 'I told you I won't use force. And if you were stringing me along, there are two edges to that sword. We'll see who's the first to get cut—and who gets cut the deepest.'

Chapter Eight

She would move, find another place to live, change her job, leave town. . . .

All night, after Tristan had gone, Larissa lay awake, planning escape. But at dawn, a calm descended on her troubled thoughts. There was no escape. She could run—but she had run before, and perhaps at nineteen that had been understandable. But now her self-respect demanded a different reaction, a less cowardly, more mature way of dealing with her own tangled emotions. She liked her job, her home. She liked living in Auckland, its warm, subtropical climate, its vitality and variety, its green parks and slumbering volcanic cones, its pretty, inviting beaches and the sprawl of its tree-filled suburbs. She liked its polyglot population of Pacific Islanders who added colour and a sort of cultural cross-pollination to the life of the city, with their music, their exotic style of dress, and relaxed lifestyles.

Dawn was streaking the sky when she fell asleep, and it seemed only minutes later that the alarm jerked her again into startled, muzzy wakefulness. But she had decided not to let Tristan panic her into flight.

She heard nothing from Tristan that week, but on the following Saturday he phoned. She put the receiver down when she heard his voice, and went out for the day, visiting friends and staying with them for dinner in the evening. She made sure it was late when she got home. On Sunday she phoned another friend and arranged to have lunch with her and visit the city art gallery for an exhibition of Pacific art.

She was home in the late afternoon, and when the phone rang she ignored it. But of course she couldn't just keep doing that. She could never be sure that it was Tristan, never know when he would turn up at the door.

Having made up her mind to face him, she found herself on tenterhooks, expecting him to contact her again. Her nerves stretched to breaking point as she waited—and waited.

He was doing it on purpose, of course. She wasn't such a fool as to believe that he had given up. He was playing with her again, deliberately keeping her in suspense, dreading his next move.

When it finally came, it was oblique and unexpected. Gemma Forbes phoned her and invited her to dinner. 'We're having a few friends,' she said. 'I think you'll like them.'

'Tristan?' Larissa enquired, her voice dry.

'Of course. He'll pick you up. You can come, I hope?'

Steadily, Larissa said, 'Thank you very much; I'd love to.'

She didn't ask if Tristan had put Gemma up to this. But the faint surprise in Gemma's pleased, 'Oh, good!' spoke for itself. Tristan had told her she might have a hard time.

She was waiting for him when he called for her. She was dressed in a calf-length printed voile frock that left her shoulders bare and hugged her closely down to the waist before swirling into a romantic, full skirt. The material was beige, splashed with misty flowers in brown and gold, with a scattering of tiny white daisies. She had pinned her dark hair high and tucked three small silk daisies into the neat chignon; slim-heeled white sandals showed off her slender feet and ankles. She knew she looked good, and what was more important, she looked poised and in command of herself. That was the impression she meant to convey, and the way she fully intended to stay.

His glance swept over her, but he didn't comment. He accompanied her down the path in silence and opened the car door for her—not the rented vehicle he had been driving before, but a larger one, dark red, low-built, with soft sheepskin seat covers.

As he got in beside her she said, 'New car?'

'Not exactly. I drove it up this week from Wellington.'

'You've been away?'

'Obviously. All week.'

She nearly laughed aloud. So he hadn't even been in town this week. All her nervous tension had been for nothing at all. Imperceptibly relaxing, she said, 'How's the new branch going?'

'Very well.'

'I'm glad.'

'Are you?' He threw her an oblique glance. 'How would you like to be my executive assistant?'

'Is that a fancy term for a secretary?'

'There would be a bit more responsibility attached. You'd have more challenging work.'

'I like the work I'm doing.'

'I thought you were a girl with ambition.'

'And I thought you didn't mix business with pleasure.'

'Changing the subject? Okay. What have you been doing this week?'

'Working,' she said dryly. 'But I went to an exhibition of Pacific art last Sunday.'

He glanced at her, betraying a flicker of interest. 'I missed that. Any good?'

She told him about it, answering his questions, and the subject kept them talking until he drew up outside a modest, weatherboard house set in a small, pretty garden.

'This is where Brian and Gemma live?' she asked.

She must have betrayed surprise. 'The boat is their only extravagance,' he said. 'They love sailing.'

The house was larger than it looked; the dining room held eight of them comfortably with the leaves of the table pulled out. The meal was delicious, the atmosphere as informal as it had been on the yacht, and there was a lot of laughter. Afterwards everyone helped to clear up and wash the dishes, and then they distributed themselves around the homely living room furnished with a rather shabby old-fashioned lounge suite and some assorted cushions, which some of the guests elected to sit on.

Larissa sat in one of the deep armchairs, and Tristan took the wide arm beside her, his hand resting on the high back of the chair, just behind her head. Coffee cups were refilled, and laughter and talk flowed freely. Larissa, listening to a lively discussion on politics, leaned her head back, and a light fingertip brushed her nape, perhaps accidentally at first, then with deliberation, in a tiny, sensual caress.

She moved slightly, drawing away, and Tristan suddenly stood up and went away from her, going across the room to speak to Brian and another man, soon deeply engrossed in conversation with them.

Gemma was collecting empty cups, and Larissa got up to help her carry them into the kitchen. She ran hot water into the sink to wash the cups while Gemma made fresh coffee. Gemma was humming to herself as she put on the percolator, a soft, secret smile curving her lips, and Larissa glanced at her and smiled herself. 'You're very happy,' she remarked.

'Blissfully,' Gemma answered, and as she looked up an inner glow seemed to emanate from her, giving her face a brief, blinding beauty. 'I'm pregnant.'

She said it with a kind of reverent glee, and Larissa laughed and said, 'Congratulations! I needn't ask if you're pleased.'

'Pleased? I've been praying for it for years. It's . . . fantastic.' She hugged herself, grinning self-consciously. 'I feel so smug it's disgusting.'

'It isn't; it's rather nice. I'm really glad for you.'

'Thanks, Larissa. You're nice. Tristan will be godfather, of course.'

Larissa, trying to imagine Tristan acting as god-father, smiled slightly. 'Is he an old friend of yours?'

'He and Brian went to school together. I never met him until after we were married. Frankly, I didn't take to him much, at first. He's a bit wary of women, not surprisingly.'

'What do you mean?'

'Have you ever met his mother?'

'Once,' Larissa answered cautiously, her attention apparently on the cup she was washing.

'I haven't,' Gemma admitted. 'But Brian's positively virulent about her—and Brian isn't normally like that; he's an easygoing soul, as a rule. According to him, Tristan's mother made his father's life unbearable and then, when he left her, she started on poor Tris. She was forever telling him how his father had no drive, no ambition, how ineffectual and unsuccessful he was, and what a mistake she had made in marrying him. And she used to laugh at Tris in front of his friends, supposedly teasing, but show-

144

ing up every little mistake he made, telling him that if he wasn't careful he would turn out like his father, that sort of thing. He was an only child, you know, and Brian says she watched him like a hawk. If he pleased her she'd give him this funny little smile and pat his cheek, and if he didn't, she was sarcastic—and sarcasm is withering to a child, especially in the adolescent stage. I remember my feelings as a teenager—too well! Can you imagine what a constant diet of that treatment would do to a sensitive boy?'

Yes, Larissa thought, she could. He would either break under it, becoming a meekly submissive nonentity, or he would learn to hide his feelings, not to give himself away. And he would learn to use the same weapons to fight back.

'Tristan is very successful,' she commented non-committally.

Gemma snorted. 'Thanks to her, I suppose,' she conceded reluctantly. 'But there's more to life than that sort of success. He isn't happy.'

'Isn't he?' Larissa took a tea towel to dry the cups, her eyes down.

'How close are you two, Larissa?' Gemma asked bluntly.

'Not very. Once'—she shrugged—'we might have been, but it didn't work out.'

'It could work out this time. He needs a nice wife and family to wipe out what his mother's done to him.'

'He doesn't want to *marry* me, Gemma,' Larissa said frankly. 'And maybe it's too late to undo anything.'

Gemma's face was a study. 'I'm fond of Tris,' she said. 'He's been a good friend to us, but don't let him hurt you, Larissa. I think he could.'

'Don't worry.' Larissa hung up the tea towel and touched the other woman's arm. 'I can look after myself. Come on; your other guests will be looking for you.'

When they came back into the lounge, Tristan looked up, and she studied his face carefully. The line of his mouth was more relaxed than usual, but his eyes as they met hers held no particular warmth, just faint, cool enquiry at her intent stare.

Inwardly sighing, she turned away. Her heart had been wrenched at the picture Gemma drew, a piercing pity for the hurt boy that he had once been, warring with a sick anger at the woman who had goaded and taunted him and made him hide behind a wall of indifference and cynicism. But the Tristan who now stood across the room was no boy, and the wall had been there a long time. Even when he had planned to marry her, he had never allowed her to penetrate it; she had only caught an occasional tantalising glimpse of what might lie behind it. And now, despising and resenting her because he believed that she had made a fool of him, laughing at his apparent stupidity just as his mother always had, he was even less likely to lower the barriers.

As he was driving her home the fantastic idea occurred to her that he might have wanted Gemma to talk to her that way. Carefully, she said, 'Tell me something; why did you ask Gemma to invite me tonight?'

He glanced at her and said, 'Actually, I didn't. It was all her own idea. She and Brian liked you and wanted to see you again.'

So she had been wrong again. Taking the plunge, she said, 'Does that mean *you* hadn't intended to see me again?'

'It doesn't follow,' he said mildly. 'I thought I had made my intentions unmistakably clear.'

'Oh, please,' she said wearily, 'please, leave me alone, Tristan.'

He didn't answer, his silence more eloquent than

words. Larissa closed her eyes tight to stop foolish tears from escaping, and didn't open them again until he drew up outside her door.

He let her out and followed her, standing close as she used her key and swung the door wide. She braced herself and turned to him, eyes wide, her face pale and defeated.

'Are you tired?' he asked her unexpectedly.

'Yes.' It was true. She felt unutterably weary and depressed.

'Good night,' he said, and his lips brushed her cheek. Then he pushed her gently into the flat and went away.

The letdown was so strong that she stood there blankly staring at the closed door for several minutes. Then, angry with herself, she whispered fiercely, 'You fool! You stupid, stupid fool! That's probably exactly what he wants you to feel. Oh, damn him! He's so clever—so horribly, diabolically clever!'

The tears came, and she didn't try to stop them. She soaked her pillow with them before she went to sleep.

She knew that Tristan was surprised when she accepted his invitation to the opening of an exhibition of contemporary Australian paintings. He had expected to have to wear her down, but Larissa decided that the best method of defence might be attack, in a modified form. Running away was predictable and easily dealt with. But if she could keep him guessing, throw him off balance, she might have a fighting chance.

No longer confused or really frightened, she knew just what she wanted. Tristan was a man she could love, perhaps the only man she would ever love. She knew that, now. But she didn't know if his mother's treatment of him had warped his character to the extent that he was incapable of loving or trusting any woman. Somehow she had to find the chink in the wall, if there was one. And it wasn't going to be easy, because if there was anything left in him that was tender or vulnerable, he would fight frantically to conceal it. Especially, perhaps, from her. Once, he had believed in her innocence, and her youth and inexperience had appealed to him. She had been no threat then. She had known nothing of the dark undercurrents in his relationship with his mother, had been much too naïve to understand what had made him the way he was. Now he had no belief in her integrity; and her ability to read him, which he had found amusing before, was a threat, because now it was more highly developed, more mature, and more effective because she knew how to use it.

Now she was a woman, with a woman's understanding, not a green young girl dazzled by a combination of worldliness, sexual expertise, and occasional careless kindness. That wasn't enough for her any more. She wanted the man beneath the armour, the reality that hid behind the mask. And she knew that if he came close to revealing his inner self she was in danger of being hurt. Her only advantage was that Tristan thought that he himself was the aggressor in this odd battle of the sexes, and she might be able, therefore, to get under his guard.

The exhibition was impressive, and since she had never lost the interest in art which he had fostered, Larissa was able to make enough confidently expressed remarks on it to provoke a stimulating discussion as Tristan drove her home.

They were still in the middle of it when he stopped the car, and he said, 'Ask me in.'

She shrugged and said, 'Come in, then.'

He concealed his surprise and followed her into the flat. She made coffee and they talked. When he put down his cup and moved purposefully towards her, pulling her out of her chair into his arms, she didn't evade him, but let him kiss her, his mouth exploratory on the softness of hers. But she didn't kiss him back, and her arms remained firmly at her sides. When he lifted his mouth to look at her with narrowed, calculating eyes, she pushed him away and walked steadily to the door, saying, 'Good night, Tristan. Thank you for taking me to the exhibition. You know how much I enjoyed it.'

For a moment he stood where he was, then he moved slowly to the door that she held open.

But it wasn't that easy. He gave the door a vicious push with the flat of his hand, and it left her fingers and slammed shut. Her eyes widened and she stepped back from him, her hands flat against the door panels as he came closer, and he said softly, 'That's not the way it's going to be, Larissa.'

Slipping his hand behind her head, he held it while he kissed her hard and long, his body pressing hers against the door, his fingers touching her ear, her throat, and running featherlightly down her arm.

Her senses were singing, heat suffusing her body, but she kept her head somehow and refused him any vestige of response. When he stopped kissing her and she saw his eyes, they steadied her, because they had not lost that hard, calculating light, and she knew he was very far from losing control.

'You're not fighting me,' he said, his eyes holding hers.

'Disappointed, Tristan?' she jibed gently. 'Is that what turns you on? The chance to subdue a frightened woman? I won't give you *that* satisfaction, either. I'm not afraid of you.'

He hauled her away from the door and kissed her again, his mouth deliberately insulting, uncaring that he bruised her lips, and his hard thigh thrust between her legs so that she had to clutch at him to keep her balance. A heady sensation of excitement rose through her being until it almost choked her, and with a tremendous effort she clenched her teeth and remained passively resistant in his arms.

At last he let her stand on her own feet, her face white but composed as his hands bit into her shoulders. He was breathing normally, but she felt the tension in his fingers on her flesh, saw the faint colour below his cheekbones. 'You want to take me to bed, Tristan?' she taunted him. 'Go ahead. I can't stop you; I'm not strong enough. But you won't enjoy it—unless you fancy making love to a statue?'

His eyes blazed briefly, making her heart stop and then resume beating much too quickly. He released her and the blaze was doused, replaced by a frigid opacity. 'Not in the mood?' he asked, with familiar mockery. 'I'm not so impatient, my dear. I can wait. But not for too long.' His eyes ran over her with an intimacy that was like a touch, an insolent careless caress. 'You're a very enticing statue,' he said, and let himself out.

It hadn't been easy, that determined resistance. After he had gone she didn't move for several minutes, and then she had to make a conscious effort to relax. When she lifted her hands there were tiny half-moon marks on her palms where her nails had driven into them. Her lips were dry and throbbing, and she felt trembly and oddly fragile. But as she prepared for bed a small, satisfied smile curved her mouth. He was a tough adversary, and he hadn't given much away. But she had at least held her own in that encounter. Altogether, she thought, the odds were about even.

She accepted other invitations from him, not all of them, but the ones which meant they were unlikely to be alone for any length of time—outings with Brian and Gemma; a play; a day swimming and surfing at Muriwai, the popular and exciting iron-sand beach, wild and unspoiled, yet within easy reach of the city. They strolled together alongside towering cliffs and crossed the gap knee-deep in waves and explored the deep cave which could be reached at low tide, then scrambled back to the beach over the cliff top, among the scrub and the tall spikes of orange-flowering flax. That day she thought that Tristan came close to being the relaxed but stimulating companion she had first known aboard the Forbes' yacht. She, too, felt less tense and more contented than she had for a long time. Superficially, lately, she had begun to know Tristan much better, his interests, his opinions, his preferences. But under the surface lay something totally different. This was nothing more than a kind of gathering of forces. Tristan was a hunter moving in for the kill, sizing up his prey before making the final, deadly strike. And she was luring him on, hoping to spring a subtle trap.

She told herself that she had the advantage because she knew exactly what Tristan wanted, whereas he couldn't possibly know her plans. She knew she had managed so far to keep him slightly off balance, just a little puzzled and unsure. They studied each other like duellists preparing for a fight to the death, each noting carefully any sign of weakness or uncertainty in the other. If he knew, when she lay unrelentingly passive under his kisses, that her indifference was a sham, she had seen the telltale tightening of his mouth that denoted his frustration. If she had to grit her teeth to survive the temptation of his caresses and found herself shaking with reaction afterwards, alone in her room, she knew that he had needed to exert an almost superhuman control to retain the mask of cynical contempt he wore when he finally released her.

It was a war of nerves, and the strain began to tell, on Larissa at least. Gemma noticed, told her she was pale, and commented on the faint shadows under her eyes. 'Been having a lot of late nights?' she asked bluntly, as Larissa helped her to wash up after supper one night.

'No more than usual.' Larissa smiled tiredly.

'Tristan looks a bit grim, too, tonight,' Gemma said. 'Have you two been fighting?'

'Fighting? Tristan never fights.'

'Doesn't he? How frustrating. But I suppose . . .'

'What?'

'Well, I gather there was plenty of fighting in the Sharpe household before his parents split up. Apparently his father had a fairly violent temper, and as I mentioned before, his mother was a shrew. Poor old Tris must have had a bellyful. Personally, I think it's a mistake for a married couple to stay together for the sake of their children, unless they can at least keep their differences private.'

'Has Tristan talked to you about it?'

'Heavens, no! I don't think he's even talked to Brian. But Brian used to spend a lot of time with Tris when they were kids. And I gather that the Sharpes weren't too choosy about who heard them snarling at each other. Of course, a lot of people seem to have the idea that children are deaf and blind as well as mentally incompetent. Haven't you ever heard mothers talking about their offspring as though the kid wasn't sitting right there, lapping up every word?'

'I've never really noticed.'

'Believe me, they do! One of my resolutions as a mum-to-be is never to do that. In fact, I shall try not to bore my friends with stories about my children at all.'

'I don't think you'll ever be a bore, Gemma.'

'Thanks. Having a baby doesn't necessarily turn one into a cabbage, I hope.'

Larissa laughed, and for some reason thought of

Helen Sharpe—bitter, waspish, and not at all motherly, with her air of brittle glamour.

'You've got the oddest look on your face,' Gemma said curiously. 'What are you thinking of?'

'Tristan's mother. Definitely not a cabbage,' Larissa said. 'But I hope you'll never be like her.'

'You've met her, you said. What was she like?'

'Rather beautiful, in a—a slightly repellent sort of way. She looks very like Tristan, blond and blue-eyed. Slim, and beautifully dressed. She had a fur on, I remember. . . .'

She recalled with sudden vivid clarity how Tristan had placed it round his mother's shoulders, and her acidly admiring comment on his deportment.

Gemma said, 'I bet she did. Tristan would have bought it for her, of course.'

'Why do you say that?'

'My dear girl, he no sooner started earning his own living than she was bleeding him for all she could get. She gets alimony from his father, but that's a pittance compared with what Tristan can provide. Tristan pays for the jam on the bread and butter. He bought her a house in Christchurch, and I believe it's quite something. It didn't cost him peanuts.'

'He said he had stopped trying to please her.'

'Did he?' Gemma looked interested. 'Well, that's new, then. He was buying jewellery for her just a couple of weeks ago.'

'How do you know?'

'Brian and I bumped into him when we were shopping for an eternity ring, and he was looking at rubies, no less, for her birthday. It seems she had expressed a preference for them.'

'Yes, I can see her in rubies,' Larissa said thoughtfully.

'I never liked them, myself,' Gemma said sourly, drying her hands with brisk thoroughness. Larissa hung up the tea towel she had been using and smiled as she followed Gemma back into the lounge to join the men.

They were looking at a small framed sketch that hung on the wall, and Gemma said, 'Oh, Brian's showing you our latest acquisition. What do you think of it, Tristan?'

'It's good,' he said. 'Where did you get it?'

While she was telling him, Brian moved away, asking Larissa if she wanted a drink.

'No, thanks,' she said. 'Who did the sketch?' She could see it was a picture of a boat harbour, done in sepia on cream paper.

'Oh, someone called Thomas—or Thompson,' he answered vaguely. 'I'm not up in these things. Gemma said it was good, and I liked it, so we bought it. Tristan knows about painting, of course. He's the frustrated artist.'

'Oh, I don't think so,' Larissa said, laughing a little. 'He's a connoisseur, I know. He likes to analyse and appreciate, but I doubt he has any ambition to try his hand himself.'

'Do you?' Brian asked rather grimly. 'Well, let me tell you, he was damned good at art back in high school. The art teacher was dead keen for him to carry on with it, and so was he, but he wasn't allowed to continue after the fourth form.'

'Why not?'

'His . . . family . . . decided there was no future in art,' Brian said with suppressed rancour. 'Math and accountancy were much more useful subjects.' He paused and smiled rather sheepishly at her. 'A lot of parents feel the same, I suppose,' he said.

'Yes.' But she was aware of a deep ache somewhere inside her, and a stirring of anger that matched Brian's unusual show of resentment. Many parents, anxious that their child should be able to find a safe, well-paying job, would have persuaded him away from a risky art career in favour of something more solidly rewarding. But, like Brian, she couldn't help feeling that in Tristan's case the decision might have had rather less to do with concern for his future comfort and welfare than for that of his mother.

Gemma and Tristan turned from their contemplation of the picture, and Gemma said lightly, 'What are you two whispering about?'

'We're not whispering,' Brian answered. 'I was just telling Larissa that Tristan used to be a pretty good artist himself. Do you still do any drawing or painting, Tris? As a hobby?'

'I've never had time for hobbies,' Tristan said colourlessly. 'No, I haven't touched a brush since . . .' He shrugged. 'Well, long before I left school.'

Rather strangely, Larissa's anger transferred itself to Tristan. 'You obviously didn't have what it takes,' she said carelessly. 'Anyone with a real artistic talent would have kept on painting, surely, even if only part-time.'

Brian muttered a surprised protest, but neither Larissa nor Tristan even glanced at him. Their eyes clashed, Larissa's lit with inexplicable temper and Tristan's deliberately expressionless.

'If I can't do a thing properly, I prefer not to do it at all,' he said. 'Art as a career—if I had chosen to pursue it—might have been something to which I could give my life. I wouldn't insult the muse'—the dry tone both acknowledged and derided the extravagance of his phrasing—'by trying to paint in my *spare time.*'

'It's a point of view,' Gemma murmured, rather bemusedly.

And Larissa said, acidly, 'In other words, if you can't be sure of achieving perfection, you won't even bother to try.'

'Not perfection,' he contradicted. 'Just a degree of . . . dedication.'

'So you've dedicated your life to making money, instead.' Her tone was deliberately scornful, and Gemma looked surprised and Brian uncomfortable and slightly alarmed. But Tristan, in his most bored tone, said, 'That's right. It gives me the means to enjoy the fruits of other people's dedication.'

Then he turned away from her to talk to Brian about something quite different, and Gemma gave Larissa a measuring glance and pursed her lips in a silent, 'Whew!'

When he took her home, she didn't invite Tristan in. She very seldom did so. As he turned her into his arms before she left the car his touch was less consciously seductive than usual, his fingers hard on her shoulders, and his kiss almost brutal.

She suffered it without flinching, and when he raised his mouth from hers she laughed softly, triumphantly. She knew that somehow, tonight, she had got under his skin a little, just a little. Somewhere she had found a nerve that still hurt when it was probed.

He heard the laugh and she felt him tauten. 'Something amuses you?' he asked her, his quiet voice holding threads of steel.

'You,' she told him. 'You're showing signs of humanity at last.'

'Because I kiss you like this?' he said, and his lips ravaged hers, quite deliberately hurtful, bruising in their impact.

Her head was bent back over his arm, and brilliant lights danced across the darkness behind her eyes. She felt his hand move in an almost rough caress over her body, and then force open the buttons of her silk blouse with scant regard for the threads that held them.

When his hand slid inside the material to touch

her skin, she whimpered a protest and clutched at his wrist, her nails digging into his flesh as she tried to stop him. He turned his hand and captured hers, holding it with his hard knuckles pressing against her breast above the low-cut edge of her bra, and his mouth continued its passionate punishment of hers.

When he took it away at last, she shut her lips tightly together to stop their trembling. They felt swollen and hot, and she whispered, 'You beast!'

'Is that what you really want?' he asked her. 'To be taken by force? So that you can pretend you didn't have a choice? Is that what you're trying to goad me into?'

'*No!*'

'It won't work,' he said, ignoring her denial. 'I'm not giving you any excuses, Larissa. You're going to admit that you want it as much as I do.'

'I thought you didn't care about that,' she said. 'I thought your money was supposed to make it worthwhile.'

'I always insist on value for money, though,' he taunted, making her clench her fists in scorching anger. 'I find it's a useful aphrodisiac.'

'I expect you've had to use it often,' she retorted bitingly. 'Your personal charm certainly isn't enough to get you what you want.'

'I've already invited you to name your price,' he reminded her.

'For what?' she said wearily. 'A body in a bed?'

'Oh, no. I want more than that. I want you, body and soul. I want your quick mind, your laughter, your sudden flashes of temper, the way you try to read what I'm thinking, with your eyes thoughtful and dark, the way you have of studying a painting with your head forward and your fingertips touching your lips. I want to hear your voice and touch your hair; I want your hand in mine and your mouth on my mouth. I want you to desire me. Yes, I want your body—but I could have taken that long ago if that was all, and you know it. It isn't nearly enough for me. I want all of you, every last bit of your being. I want it all!'

Larissa didn't know if she was angry or surprised, moved or faintly amused. She heard the unbelievable words in the unemotional voice, and had a strong desire to weep. In the end, she said quite gently, 'But Tristan, the price of *that*—is marriage.'

Chapter Nine

She sensed his sudden wary withdrawal and wondered if he was realising how close he had come to giving himself away. When he spoke, his voice had the familiar sardonic note. 'You haggle brilliantly, darling, but I'm still not prepared to offer that much.'

It hurt, as he had meant it to, but she wouldn't let him know that. 'You really are pathetic,' she said, witheringly. 'You can't think of anything except in terms of its market value, can you? Do you really imagine you can put a price on love?'

'I'm not talking about love,' he said harshly.

'What, then?' she asked, the smile on her lips almost tender.

'I thought you disliked crudity. If you want it put bluntly, I'm talking about what return you would require in exchange for your time and certain services rendered.'

'How much of my time did you have in mind?'

'I don't know,' he admitted curtly.

'I see. It would depend on when you grew tired of my . . . services, would it?'

'Obviously.' He bit off the word, his expression

coldly bored, as though anticipating a time when he would have had enough of Larissa Lovegrove, perhaps be relieved to get rid of her.

'And you'd pay me off—generously?' she enquired softly.

His eyes narrowed a little, gleaming at her in the darkness. 'Are you ready to talk terms?'

He didn't really think so; he was calling her bluff, putting an end to her baiting because he suspected she was teasing him, and he didn't like it.

'No,' she said. 'I'm not ever going to talk terms with you, Tristan. I just wanted this . . . proposition of yours put into words in the hope that you might realise just how much of an arrogant, mercenary, inhuman beast you are. If you honestly think that you can buy emotions and bargain with people's feelings, I think you're beyond hope.'

'Hope of what? Were you planning to reform me?'

That was pretty smart of him, she thought dispassionately. But Tristan had always been quick.

'Reform?' she said lightly. 'You flatter yourself, I'm afraid. I just want you to leave me alone.'

'No chance. And if you really want that, why do you accept my invitations?'

'Because if I didn't you'd make a nuisance of yourself, and you know very well that your invitations are often interesting in themselves.'

'And that's all?' His tone was ironic.

Calmly, she said, 'You can be good company when you put yourself out a little. You must be aware that you're a useful and presentable escort. And at least we do know where we stand. You want to get me into bed, and I have no intention of obliging you. It makes for . . . simplicity, anyway.'

She hoped she sounded cool and slightly squashing, and that she had succeeded in shaking him, however little. It would do him good. And she also hoped that she had distracted him thoroughly from the dangerous topic of what she really wanted from him.

When she opened the door of the car, he didn't detain her, and she wondered if she had given him some food for thought.

After that evening, though, she changed her tactics, coolly and adamantly refusing all his invitations. It was risky, of course, but she was sure he had been about to change his own strategy, knowing that Tristan never endured a stalemate for long. Pursuing her policy of keeping him off balance, she decided to take the initiative herself, even if it was in a negative direction.

When he came to the flat and pushed the door open against her expected resistance, closing it behind him, she looked at him with wary expectancy.

There was no sign of temper in his face, and she turned from him and silently sat down with her head tilted in defiant challenge, her emotions a mixture of chagrin and relief. He was going to be difficult and unpleasant, concealing any hint of his real feelings, armoured against her.

'I have neighbours, you know,' she said. 'I could scream.'

'You told me that before,' he said indifferently. He knew she wouldn't scream, of course. This was between the two of them, and although technically he had forced his way into her home, she had no intention of letting him know she was in any way frightened.

'Well?' she said, looking up into the cold mask of his face.

'You know why I'm here.'

'Because I won't go out with you any more. I got tired of playing mouse to your cat, Tristan. I'm opting out.'

'You're scared,' he jeered softly.

'Scenting victory?' she said, so dryly that he went still, his eyes riveted on her face. 'What an egoist, you are,' she went on. 'You're wrong. This is no last-ditch stand. I have simply had enough.'

'I haven't.'

She looked at the cold brilliance of his eyes, the determined set of his mouth, and said, clearly, 'I will not dance to your tune, Tristan. You will *never* make me your mistress. You'll just have to accept that.'

'I never accept defeat.'

'It will be a new experience for you. Finding out that *people* can't be manipulated for your convenience like a column of figures.'

He hadn't sat down, but was standing quite close to her, tall and very still. It was late afternoon, and the sun slanted in one of the windows and burnished the smoothness of his hair. His dark trousers clung to his hips, and his thin white shirt seemed to be moulded to him.

Larissa smiled, suddenly amused. 'You look very Greek god-ish,' she said. 'Are you striking a pose for my benefit?'

Something in his face changed, and he suddenly stooped, and with unbelievable grace and strength, lifted her right out of the chair and into his arms. He was striding through to her bedroom before she had time to recover her wits, and even as she made a surprised, furious swipe at his face, he dropped her down on the bed and held her there as he joined her.

Larissa made one instinctive, convulsive effort at escape, which he stopped easily, his hands on her wrists, forcing them down on the pillow, his body trapping hers.

She looked into his eyes, quivered and went rigid, and then made herself relax, but every nerve screamed at the nearness of him, the strength in his long fingers, the cool determination in his eyes.

'*What do you think you're doing?*' she demanded from between clenched teeth, her voice low because she wanted to scream it at him, a shrill, frightened cry.

A strange light came and went in the blue depths of his eyes. 'I'm going to make love to you,' he said. 'Until you beg for mercy.'

'You can't!' she gasped, panic edging her voice.

'Can't? Who's going to stop me? Your friendly neighbours aren't home, didn't you know? All the windows are shut, and there are no cars. Besides, you weren't really going to scream, were you?'

His mouth stopped her answer before it left her tongue. His kiss drowned all thought for a time, only the firm, but unexpectedly tender demands of his mouth filling her mind. Coherent thought scattered as he parted her lips beneath his, his mouth a seduction in itself, the length of his body against her a terrifying temptation to passion.

His mouth left hers and began a slow passage down her throat. Her dress was a synthetic, halter-necked affair, thin and silky and cut low between her breasts, and his mouth soon found the shadowed hollow there, his tongue flicking fire over the soft, exposed curves.

Larissa stirred restlessly and whispered a strangled, '*Don't!*' but he wouldn't stop. She struggled desperately, trying to get a purchase on the bed with her foot, but as she raised her knee the dress slid back to the top of her thigh, and when Tristan lifted his head, it was only to look at the line of her leg, uncovered for him to see. He released one of her hands to slide his fingers from her knee to her hip, slipping under the dress, finding the narrow strip of the bikini briefs she was wearing and the warm smooth skin beyond.

The hand that he had freed moved to stop him,

and, surprisingly, he let her push his intruding fingers away, smiling and catching her wrist again to press kisses along the sensitive skin of her inner arm.

He kissed her again on the mouth, a long, deep, desirous kiss that made her dizzy with pleasure, and she closed her eyes and willed herself not to put her arms about him, not to run her fingers over his shoulders as he was doing to hers.

He kissed her shoulders too, and, still holding her hand, thrust it inside his opened shirt, making her feel the astonishing smoothness of the tanned skin over his ribs, pressing her palm over the deep, steady beat of his heart, bringing her fingertips down to feel the taut stomach above the heavy buckle of his belt.

She snatched her hand away then, horrified at the images which coursed unbidden into her brain. Tristan made a soft sound of satisfaction and shifted suddenly, his hands firmly turning her away from him onto her side, but his arm beneath her held her against him, his hand against her waist, spreading fingers over her stomach as his mouth roamed over her shoulders and down the column of her spine where the sundress was cut almost to waist level. His free hand caressed her arm, then wandered to her thigh and slid upwards. Larissa made a jerky movement of protest, and his soft laughter came to her ear as he shifted his hand back to her waist and began to explore from there, softly touching the swell of her breast and then retracing the path down to her hip.

'Tristan,' she whispered, 'Stop this. You must stop!'

He ignored her, his hands and his mouth doing crazy things to her equilibrium, making her feel weightless, drugged. She knew she should be fighting him, but the will to resist was ebbing fast, was almost nonexistent now. She wanted him so much;

nothing else in the wide world seemed to matter. If only this sweet, marvellous, exciting loving could go on. . . .

She couldn't see his face, and she shifted in his arms, trying to turn onto her back. He lifted his head, and just as she turned, looking up at him, his eyes went past her to the photograph that stood on the bedside table, only a snapshot in a cheap plastic holder, not very big, but certainly close enough for him to recognise the face.

He said nothing, but she felt the sudden rigid stillness of his body and saw his face go taut, the mouth draw into a hard straight line, the eyes narrow suddenly. His hand passed over her shoulders and his fingers found the tie that secured the halter top of her dress. He tugged at it with purpose, and she felt the thin strings part and put up a hand to stop him from pulling them down, holding the material over her breasts.

He pushed her hands impatiently aside, and she was staring now into his eyes, implacable and stony, not loving at all, but hating, hating her and wanting to hurt. . . .

'No,' she whispered. 'Oh, no! Tristan, please . . . oh, *please*. . . .'

She felt his hand on the flimsy material, the warm scrape of his knuckles against her skin, and she closed her eyes against the terrible look in his and felt the hot tears squeeze from under her lids.

He was silent and still, and time seemed to tick by forever. Shame twisted inside her, shame and humiliation and dreadful heartbreak. She twisted her head away, trying to hide the tears from him, and then she felt the tiny bodice being pulled into place again, and the bed lightened as he got off and left her lying there.

She wiped a hand across her eyes and opened

them. Tristan was standing by the bed, with the snapshot in his hand, looking at it. 'Jeffrey,' he said. 'Do you still see him?'

She sat up and fumblingly tied the halter neck at her nape, her fingers shaking. 'Now and then,' she said warily. 'He's a sailor.'

He laughed, shortly, unpleasantly, and said, 'Among other things.'

It should have made her angry, but she felt dull and weary now. 'Please go,' she said.

He turned the frame to examine the back, slipped the photograph out and, replacing the frame on the table, slowly and deliberately tore the snapshot in two. With the pieces held in one hand, he said, 'Why did you cry?'

The anger came then, healing, cauterising, hot and sharp. 'Perhaps,' she said viciously, 'because you're not Jeffrey!'

She didn't want to look at him, but her eyes remained fascinated by the torn pieces in his hand. They were crumpled suddenly in his fist, and then he threw them in her lap. 'Did Jeffrey ever make you beg, Larissa?' he asked. And then he walked out.

She heard him close the outer door and put her head in her hands, rocking back and forth to ease the pain, a deep hurt somewhere in her chest, a physical agony that seemed unendurable. He had said he would make her beg for mercy, and that was just what he had done. And once he had achieved that he had been able to stop and go away. *He* hadn't been carried away, mindless with delight, lifted into another dimension where old hatreds and old misunderstandings didn't matter any more. He had been waging a battle campaign, his brain never losing sight of the objective—the subjugation of the woman who had said she didn't want him. He hadn't even lost his temper one iota when he tore the photograph of Jeffrey. It hadn't been done in a fit of blind, jealous rage, but slowly and methodically, simply because he had thought she would be hurt by it.

He was inhuman, a cold-blooded monster without normal feelings, someone whose heart had been cut from his body long ago or had frozen so deeply it couldn't be thawed. All he had left was his pride and the ability to defend it with an implacable desire for vengeance.

And she had thought she could get close to a man like that! Thought she could repair the damage that had been done in childhood and confirmed by events in his adult life. How pathetic such an ambition seemed now! Sometimes it had seemed almost within her grasp, the warm, eager pulsing life that once had been, before the ice took over and froze his normal human reactions. Sometimes she had seemed so close to finding the man behind the mask. Thought that he was coming close to loving her, even though his conscious mind rejected the idea. But it hadn't been loving at all, that slow, sweet wooing of her body this afternoon. It had only been a matter of technique, a cynical show of sexual power calculated to bring her to her knees because she had laughed at him and he couldn't bear to be laughed at.

One of the good things about her job was the fact that she could take a week off virtually at will. She did it now, taking up a standing offer which one of her neighbours had made, of the use of his fishing cottage near Rotorua. The lake was tranquil; the secluded little bay where the cottage nestled among a tangle of kahikatea, tree ferns, and fragrant tarata at the water's edge was a haven of quiet. There was a natural hot spring close by, only yards from where cool, crystal-clear water bubbled from the ground and formed a pool big enough for swimming. The hot spring provided water for a bath when she wanted it, and each day she had a dip in the cold pool, the water so fresh and pure she felt tingling with life afterwards. She watched the trout jumping in the lake and explored the lakeside bush, careful to keep to the paths worn smooth over the white pumice because the little columns of steam that rose here and there through the trees denoted thermal activity, small boiling pools of mud or water, and an unwary step on the thin crust of the earth might mean falling into one of them. The smell of sulphur pervaded the air, but one got used to that quite quickly; after the first day she didn't notice it.

But the quiet and the solitude were perhaps a mistake. Her thoughts pursued her; there was no escape from the memories and the regrets, and she went into the city one day and spent the morning shopping, buying clothes she didn't need, and combing the souvenir shops for some good Maori carvings to take home for various friends. In the afternoon she took a launch trip to the island of Mokoia in the centre of Lake Rotorua and listened idly as the tour guide detailed the love story of Tutanekai and Hinemoa, the lovers who were parted by intertribal conflict and reunited by Hinemoa's bravery in swimming from the lake shore to the island, following the sound of Tutanekai's flute as he played it on the island. Life should be so simple, she thought, and, looking about the crowd on the boat, saw the number of honeymooning couples with their arms about each other, the soft smiles on their faces, and realised that this trip had been another mistake.

She had hoped to gain a breathing space, some time to gather strength to make a final and irrevocable break with Tristan. If there was no future in their relationship—and common sense told her there wasn't—she had to sever it cleanly and swiftly. The trouble was, she didn't know how to make him accept that.

She expected to hear from him as soon as she returned, but for a whole week there was no word or sign of him. Perhaps he had finally given up, she thought, and the depression that entered her soul at that thought made her furious with herself. It simplified matters, didn't it? No need for a repudiation scene or laboured explanations, an attempt to batter at his cool determination with either logic or anger. If he had decided to admit defeat and give up his vengeful pursuit, so be it.

But she couldn't help recalling the implacable way he had told her that he never accepted defeat, and she waited uneasily for another move from him.

When it came it was shatteringly unexpected. He drew up in his car at her usual bus stop after work one evening, and weak-mindedly, as she afterwards told herself, she allowed him to almost force her into accepting a lift home because she couldn't withstand the stares of the other people waiting at the stop while she argued with him. He hauled her into the car with a hard hand on her wrist, in the end, and she put up only a token struggle.

'It would serve you right if they called the police,' she muttered angrily, rubbing her wrist as he turned the car into the stream of traffic.

'It had more the appearance of a lovers' quarrel than an abduction,' he said. 'Why didn't you want to come?'

'I don't want to see you again!'

He glanced at her but said nothing, and they drove the rest of the way in stony silence. When he stopped the car she said, 'Thanks for the lift,' and got out, but he was right beside her as she went up the path to her front door.

'Can't you take a hint?' she asked him, pausing on the step.

'Stop quibbling,' he said. 'I'm coming in. I want to . . . say something to you.'

'Then say it here.'

'No.'

'Look, I'm tired and it's hot, and I want to freshen up and eat and have a nice restful evening.'

'Go ahead. I won't stop you.'

She turned her back on him and used her key, and when he followed her and closed the door behind him she ignored him and went into the bedroom, kicked off her shoes and dropped her bag, then locked herself in the bathroom.

She deliberately took a long time showering in lukewarm water, smoothing scented talc over her body and brushing her hair out before she pinned it up casually in a loose knot. She pulled on a cool silk caftan that Jeffrey had brought back for her from Singapore, its jewel-bright colours of green, blue, and deep red emphasising the darkness of her eyes. It was what she would have worn if Tristan had not been there, but she was aware that the gossamer-soft silk clung lightly where it touched her breasts and hips, skimming over her waist and flaring about her legs and outlining them when she walked.

Tristan had not sat down; he was staring out the window at the lacy canopy of the jacaranda when she came into the lounge and crossed to the kitchen bar. He turned and watched her, and when she had taken a steak out of the small freezer compartment of her refrigerator, she asked reluctantly, 'Do you want to eat with me?'

'Thank you,' he said gravely.

'Don't thank me,' she said tartly. 'The only thing worse than having to eat with you would be having to eat alone with you watching me!'

He laughed, and she involuntarily looked up at him. He laughed wholeheartedly so seldom that it surprised her, and she felt a peculiar wrenching in her heart when she saw how it transformed his features into something much more human and less harsh than his usual expression.

'Can I help?' he offered, and she said curtly, 'No thanks.' She turned away from him to unwrap the steak and find a broiler pan.

He didn't offer again, and when she put the two plates on the table, he pulled out her chair for her in silence and then sat opposite, apparently enjoying the succulent steak and the salad she had prepared to go with it.

'I remember what a good cook you are,' he said at last, pushing away his empty plate. 'I do believe your cooking saved my life, once.'

Extravagant phrases were very unlike him. She shot him a quick glance, finding his mouth curled in mockery. 'Your life was in no danger,' she said crisply. 'And you were probably so hungry you wouldn't have noticed what sort of meal it was.'

'Oh, no!' he contradicted immediately. 'Until you came along I hadn't even realised that I *was* hungry.'

She suspected a hidden meaning there, something in his voice sounded both intimate and derisive. She pushed back her chair and said, 'I don't usually have dessert, but there's some tinned fruit if you'd like it.'

'No, thanks.' He watched her take their plates and, as she began making coffee, strolled over to the counter to watch her.

'Thanks,' he said as she handed him his filled cup. He took it over to the sofa and sat down, and although she would have preferred to drink it at the table, it would have looked silly, so she sat at the other end and sipped her coffee in silence, not looking at him.

He finished first, and when she had drunk hers he leaned over and took her cup from her, placing it on the side table where he had put his own.

'Don't look so wary,' he said. 'I'm not going to leap on you.'

'What did you want to say to me?' she asked him.

'A sort of replay of history,' he murmured, and she saw his mouth twist bitterly. Then he said, 'On second thought, it's too damned ludicrous to repeat the words. This will say it all.'

He took a small box from his pocket, and even as her eyes widened and her breath caught in shock, he deftly took the ring from it and caught her left hand to slide the glittering band onto her finger.

It was a diamond cluster so large and ostentatious that it almost reached the knuckle of her finger. It glittered harshly at her, and when she looked up she saw the same hard glitter in his eyes, the blue almost washed out of them.

'You win,' he said softly, releasing her hand. And Larissa, suddenly emerging from a shock-induced stupor, swung back her hand and hit him as hard as she could.

She jumped up, flushed with fury, and he followed, facing her with the red mark of her hand on his cheek and his mouth tight. 'Well,' he said, 'it's a novel way of receiving a proposal of marriage.'

'*You beast!*' she cried. 'You rotten, lousy swine! I told you I'm *not* for sale!'

'On the contrary,' he interrupted coolly, 'you set a price on yourself—which I'm now willing to pay.'

'You know I didn't mean it,' she whispered, her horrified eyes on his face. 'You *know* I didn't!'

'Didn't you? You may not have thought I'd bid that high, but you hoped, all right. Why else did you keep seeing me? Don't tell me I forced you to,' he added as she took a swift breath, her lips parting on

172

a stinging retort. 'You could have just kept saying no—but you didn't.'

Because I love you! her heart cried at last. But she couldn't say it aloud. He would laugh in her face.

'It's the best offer you're likely to get, Larissa,' he said tauntingly. His eyes went to the ring he had placed on her finger. 'That's only a sample of what I can provide for you, after we're married.'

The word made her heart lurch. For a moment she was horribly tempted. Maybe, if she accepted, in time he would come to realise how he had misjudged her and wronged her . . . Maybe she could prove to him that she wasn't just a mercenary little cheat after all. But her pride revolted at the thought of marrying him on his terms, and her soul shuddered when she envisaged the future if she couldn't make him believe in her. Years, perhaps a lifetime, of Tristan's bitter contempt and his reluctant desire.

'No,' she said. 'Oh, no!'

'Don't be a little fool!' Tristan said with sharp exasperation. 'What do you want? I'm not going to beg, if that's what you're hoping for.'

'You're the fool, Tristan,' she said clearly, suddenly ablaze again with anger. 'I have no intention of marrying you, now, or ever. I won't be your mistress, and I won't marry you. I don't think I ever want to see you again. Now,' she said, tugging off the ring, and holding it out to him. 'Will you please go, and take your horrible, vulgar bauble with you!'

She saw the answering blaze in his eyes and recoiled instinctively from it, but it was too late. His hands pulled her violently against him, and his mouth descended on hers with such force that her lips were crushed into numbness. She fought him desperately, but he was uncaring if he hurt her, his fingers biting cruelly into her flesh, his breathing harsh as his mouth at last left hers to press hot, angry kisses against her throat, pushing back the collar of her caftan so roughly that she heard the fine material tear and branding her with a long, open-mouthed kiss against the gentle swell of her breast.

When at last she fought free, she hit him again—and then again. His lips were drawn back from his teeth a little, like a snarl, and his eyes glittered with barely contained rage.

She stumbled back from him and went towards the door. 'Get out!' she said, almost sobbing, her hand reaching for the knob.

He came up behind her saying her name and, holding her arm, twisted her to face him. Larissa lashed out again, her hand glancing off the side of his jaw as he jerked his head aside.

'Stop it, you little bitch,' he said gratingly, and she found herself slammed back against the wall by the door, his hands holding her so that there was no escape.

'Let me go!' She kicked out at him, but her bare feet made no impression on the hardness of his shin, and he suddenly shook her, making her dizzy, and then pushed her back to the wall.

Panting, she glared back at him, and the expression on his face jolted her into sudden panic. His eyes were slitted, his skin seemed to be stretched over the bone beneath, and with the marks of her blows fading, he looked strangely pale. He was making a tremendous effort to control himself; even his voice was husky with it. 'Is this what you've been angling for?' he asked grimly. 'You've been leading me up the garden path, waiting for me to capitulate, so that you could have the pleasure of turning me down—is that it?'

She never knew what made her say it, what gave her the courage to do something so mad, so patently dangerous. There was anger in her, and fear, but there was also still that driving need to finally strip off the mask, and she knew he was close to breaking point now. Closer than he had ever been.

She looked into his eyes and managed a smile, a slow, feline smile of triumph. 'Yes,' she said. 'Yes, Tristan. I've got what I wanted—and it's a sweet vengeance.'

Fascinated, she saw his face change. It was like watching a film where a camera trick replaced one face with another. Dark colour flooded his skin, and his eyes opened wider, the pupils shrinking as the irises seemed to blaze into incandescent fury. His jaw thrust out and his teeth snapped together, as between them he said hoarsely, 'God *damn* you to hell, Larissa!'

And one of his hands left her shoulder, curled into a fist, raised, and as her eyes snapped wide open in terrified disbelief, watching the movement, it smashed down again towards her. It was as though everything happened in slow motion for those few seconds, and she seemed paralysed, unable to do anything. But when that fist began its downward swing she suddenly screamed and desperately flung herself aside, only to be stopped by the hard arm that was in her path, where Tristan still had his other hand flattened against the wall beside her.

She heard the tremendous thud and a cracking sound, and felt the wall vibrate behind her back. Then there was silence except for her own sobbing breaths, and Tristan's, loud and harsh sounding, close to her ear. She realised that she had flung a hand up against her face, trying to protect herself, and she waited, huddled, for the next blow.

It didn't come, and after a heart-stopping moment she dared to move, to lower her hand and slowly, slowly, turn her head.

There as a jagged hole in the plaster of the wall, torn wallpaper holding pieces of it, and a shower of white fragments on the floor. The hole was at least eighteen inches from where her head had been, and at last she raised her eyes to his face, terror changing to puzzlement.

He looked—shattered. There wasn't another word for it. He was pale again, and his eyes registered shock—shock and incredulity. He looked down at his hand and flexed the fingers. There was a smear of blood across the knuckles, mingled with white plaster dust. Then he looked up again into her eyes, eyes that were still shocked and questioning. 'My God,' he said softly, so softly she could scarcely hear. 'You thought I meant to hit you, didn't you?'

Her throat felt raw, and her first attempt to speak was unsuccessful. Then she managed a shaky whisper. 'Yes.'

He shook his head, almost helplessly, and closed his eyes, his face suddenly twisting into a mask of anguish. 'Don't you know,' he said unsteadily, 'I love you too much to even think of that?'

'Darling!' she said softly. 'Darling . . .' And her arms went round him, pulling his fair head down to her for comfort, her lips against his cheek.

His arms came about her convulsively, his embrace so tight she could scarcely breathe, and his lips were on the curve of her neck, almost feverish with his naked need.

And then a thunderous knocking came at the door, a man's voice shouting anxiously, 'Larissa? Are you all right in there?'

For a moment they clung together. Then the shout came again, and she stirred reluctantly, pulling away from him. She went swiftly to open the door. 'It's all right, Stan. I'm fine,' she said as calmly as she could.

'We heard a scream,' he said, his face reflecting an odd mixture of belligerence and embarrassment as he looked past her and saw Tristan standing within the room.

'I'm sorry,' she said. 'It was awfully good of you to come and investigate. I feel a fool, but there was this spider . . .'

'We heard a thump, too,' Stan muttered stubbornly. He started a little as he sidled into the doorway and saw the hole torn in the wall. 'Sure you're okay?' he reiterated anxiously. He now stood between her and Tristan, uncertain, but bulky and prepared to usher her out if she needed rescuing.

Touched by his concern, she smiled at him. 'I saw a spider—a huge thing—and when I screamed Tristan rather overreacted, I'm afraid. He certainly disposed of the spider, though.'

She managed a little laugh, and after a moment Stan joined in. His glance at Tristan was friendly now, but still slightly puzzled. 'Well . . . sorry to barge in,' he said at last.

'That's all right, Stan. I'm grateful. . . .'

'It's good to know that Larissa's neighbours are concerned for her,' Tristan said behind her. 'Thanks.'

Stan left, dismissed by that quiet, cool courtesy of Tristan's, and she closed the door behind him and turned.

The mask was back in place, not a vestige of emotion in his expression; it was exactly like his voice, courteous—and cold.

Irritation flared for a moment, and then she smiled at him, allowing tenderness and humour and love to blend in the look she gave him. After all, nothing could erase those few minutes when she had finally succeeded in tearing the mask off, but of course he didn't feel safe without it, not yet.

'You proved a point there,' he said, one hand carelessly shoved into his pocket as he moved an ornament on the mantel with the other, and replaced it with care.

She raised her brows in silent query, and he explained, 'You told me the neighbours would come running if you ever screamed. I'm surprised you didn't try it on some other occasions.'

'Perhaps I didn't really want to,' she admitted quietly.

His look was penetrating, and she went over to him and put her arms about his waist, tipping back her head to look at him, her eyes brilliant. 'I love you,' she said. 'I think I always did.'

She saw the derision in his smile before he put his hands on hers and quite gently, but firmly, removed them. Then he walked away from her, and with his back to her said, 'No, you didn't. You had an adolescent crush on me, which I deliberately encouraged.'

She might have argued with that, but instead she said, 'Did you? Why?'

He half turned to throw a glance at her, and then he turned away again and said deliberately, 'Because I wanted you, and I knew that with a minimum of sexual expertise I could make you want me—you were ready to fall in love, and I knew that. I wanted it to be me. I—desperately—wanted it to be me.'

'*Desperately?*'

'Yes.' He suddenly swung round, and there was a kind of latent hostility in his face. 'I'd never been in love in my life, and it had to be an infant like you! A teenager who didn't even know what life was about. It was too ridiculously easy to make you think that you loved me.'

Slightly stung, she said, 'Was it?'

'You know it was. That evening I made you stay and cook a meal for us both, you were no more in love with me than with your office desk, until I kissed you once or twice, and then you'd have said anything—done anything—for me.'

She remembered the derision in his voice when

she had told him that night that she loved him, and
he had replied, 'Of course.'

'You didn't ask me to do—anything,' she reminded him.

'I asked you to marry me.'

'So you did. Why did you decide that was necessary?' she asked with slight irony.

'I was *in love* with you, dammit!'

Larissa laughed, and something flickered in his
eyes, leaving them a shade warmer. 'I was scarcely
aware of it,' she said, 'You were just as inclined
to snap my head off at times as to kiss my breath
away.'

'I had to,' he said strangely.

Larissa shook her head. 'Had to what?'

'Keep you slightly on edge all the time, because if
you were a little angry with me, it kept you from
falling into my arms, where I wanted you to be. I
know I tried to rush the wedding, but at least I had
enough decency left to leave you a way out—not to
force you to commit yourself to me without a legal
ceremony to protect you.'

'From you?'

'From your own doubts about my . . . intentions.'

A smile tugged at her mouth, and he said rather
harshly, 'And I wasn't quite such a louse that I'd
seduce an innocent, even one I was planning to
marry.'

'You're really very gallant in your own strange
way, aren't you, Tristan?' she said, gently teasing.

'Too much so, perhaps,' he said, his mouth twisting suddenly. 'While I was walking a tightrope
between making love to you just enough to make
you eager for more, and ensuring that you never
became sentimental enough to tempt me to break
my good resolutions, it didn't occur to me that I was
paving the way for some brash young idiot to get you
into bed.'

Her smile stiffened and disappeared. Jeffrey. The name hovered unspoken in the air between them.

'Paved the way?' she repeated.

His look was impatient. 'I was deliberately keeping you in a state of sexual tension. And at the same time making you dislike me intensely at times—do you think I didn't know that? For anyone who offered you a shoulder to cry on, or even a straight-out uncomplicated one-night stand, you must have been a pushover.'

'Thank you,' she said through pale lips. 'Considering your opinion of my character, I'm surprised you could bring yourself to fancy marrying me.'

He looked almost nonplussed. Then a faint line of colour darkened his cheekbones. 'I'm sorry,' he said. 'But it's the only way I can make any sense of—' He stopped, made a strange, abrupt little gesture with his hand, and Larissa said, 'Of my sleeping with Jeffrey? But I never did, Tristan. Never. Not with Jeffrey. Not with anyone, as a matter of fact.'

She spoke very calmly, with an odd conviction that, really, it didn't matter whether he believed her or not. And his look, too, seemed quite indifferent. But then he said, 'Not even—since?'

Larissa shook her head, a faint smile on her lips.

'Didn't it occur to you,' he asked rather carefully, 'in recent weeks, that there's a rather easy way of proving that?'

'Yes. It did occur to me. Are you going to ask me to prove it?'

'No.'

He came over to her, his eyes holding hers, and put out a hand, touching her hair in an almost tentative way. He twisted a strand about his fingers, and looking at it, not at her face, he said quite mildly, 'Who the devil *is* Jeffrey, anyway?'

'My foster-brother,' she said. 'I'd like him to be at the wedding, if you don't mind.'

'Wedding?' His eyes lifted sharply to hers, wary and cool.

Larissa smiled, put up a hand to his as it held her hair, and turned to kiss the scraped skin on his knuckles. His fingers tightened suddenly and tugged until she had to turn her face up to him. 'You said you wouldn't—' he reminded her.

'That was before . . .' she said, her eyes shining fearlessly into his. 'It's a woman's privilege to change her mind. Unless the offer has been withdrawn?'

He actually winced before he took her in his arms.

Chapter Ten

Jeffrey reacted rather grimly when she told him who she was marrying. He hadn't forgotten the traumatic experience of his first meeting with Tristan Sharpe. But the small wedding went off smoothly, in spite of Jeffrey's stiffness and Tristan's mother's scarcely veiled barbs. Larissa kept on smiling through it all, and Tristan assumed his most bored expression but kept up an appearance of half-mocking civility to everyone. Only with Brian and Gemma did he drop his guard, giving them one of his rare grins, and occasionally when he looked at Larissa she detected the warmth lurking in his blue eyes that was specially for her.

When it was all over and they were speeding south in Tristan's car, bound for Taupo and a cottage by the lake, Larissa fingered the wide, engraved gold band on her finger and sighed with relief.

'What's that for?' Tristan demanded. 'Sorry already?'

'Of course not. Just glad that we're alone—and together.'

'That sounds nice,' he murmured, and she saw the crease in his cheek that meant he was holding back a smile. On impulse, she leaned over and kissed it, and his hands tightened on the wheel until the knuckles were white as he said calmly, 'It's dangerous to distract the driver.'

She watched his hands graudally lose their tension with calm satisfaction, a tiny smile on her own lips. She was learning to read this enigmatic man of hers, becoming an expert on the small giveaways which most people never noticed. When he was emotionally moved he pretended to be thoroughly bored, and that flat tone of voice meant he was controlling himself with great deliberation. He was sarcastic if anyone threatened to get close to his inner self, the self he tried to hide even from her. But the first cracks in the ice had already appeared, and they would get wider every day. One day, she promised herself, the avalanche.

It came sooner than she had expected. That night the floodgates opened, in tenderness and in passion, in whispered words of love and need, and in a final triumphant cry of abandoned joy. Even in the drowsy aftermath he went on murmuring to her, 'I love you, I love you . . . you are my life, my soul . . . nothing existed for me before you. . . .'

She stroked his face in wonder and pulled his head down on her breast, touching his hair, until he shifted in the bed and began kissing her shoulders and throat softly, and, brushing his lips against her cheek, found the tears there.

'Why?' he whispered softly. 'Did I hurt you? I'm sorry, my darling, I tried not to.'

She shook her head. 'No—no. It isn't that.'

'What, then?' he insisted, tasting the salt tears, licking them away. 'Tell me.'

At the faintly imperious note, she smiled in the darkness. 'Because,' she said, 'I know you now.'

'In the biblical sense?' he asked, faintly puzzled, and therefore sounding very dry.

'Mmm,' she murmured noncommittally. She meant more than that. In the morning he would don the mask once more, but never again would he be able to hide from her. The knowledge she had gained tonight could never be forgotten or erased. But she would not abuse it. She would use it skilfully and with love, not to hurt or belittle him or to manipulate him for her own selfish needs and desires, but to help him, to bring him gradually into the light of the love and friendship and concern of other people, so that he didn't need the mask so often.

'Trust,' she whispered. 'I'll teach you how to trust again, my dearest lover.'

'I do trust you,' he said, and her heart turned over with love because he sounded almost sulky, like the boy he had once been. 'You know I do,' he insisted.

'Yes,' she soothed. 'I know.'

He had shown that trust conclusively, in the last few weeks, by putting a deliberate restraint on his lovemaking, just as he had years ago, but this time she understood his reason as she had never understood then. He wanted her to know, unequivocally, that he was not asking for proof of her innocence.

'You have your proof now,' she reminded him gently.

Immediately, he stiffened in her arms. 'I don't need it, I told you,' he said forcibly. 'Did you think I still doubted the truth?'

'I thought—there might have been a nagging little reservation at the back of your mind.'

'There wasn't. That night, I knew you were telling me the truth at last.'

There was a pause, and he was still tense, and when he burst out with the question, she knew he had promised himself never to ask it. But the pain behind it would not be denied its answer. '*Why*— why did you tell me, when you broke our engagement, that Jeffrey was your lover?'

'I'm so sorry,' she whispered. 'I'm so sorry. I was frightened.'

'Of *me?*'

He was no longer guarding his tone, concealing his feelings behind mockery or boredom. He sounded astonished.

'You're a pretty scary person,' she said.

'I never scared *you!*' he said. 'I made you laugh.'

Surprised, she said, 'Yes, you did, sometimes. Did you mind very much?'

'You thought I was a stuffed shirt who needed deflating,' he said.

'No!'

'Yes. And you set out to do it. But without malice. No one had ever treated me like that before—laughing at me, but with tenderness. Bullying me with gentleness and consideration. Standing up to my foul moods with a temper of her own.'

'*I* bullied you? As if—'

'Yes, as if,' he teased. 'What else did you do, when I was sick that time?'

'Well—that didn't last long.'

'Long enough for me to realise I was crazily in love with you.'

'Crazily?' Her voice shook. 'You hid it very well.'

'I was afraid of you,' he said abruptly. Then, rather fiercely, he repeated, 'Yes, *I* was afraid of *you!*'

'Afraid that I'd hurt you?' she queried softly.

'I thought I'd found a reason for my fear when I saw you with Jeffrey,' he admitted harshly. 'I knew I'd been a brute to you; I'd spent the entire weekend trying to contact you to apologise, and then—it seemed you'd taken your revenge in the most painful way possible.'

Her hands tightened about his neck, and he said roughly, 'Is that why you told me that lie? Because you were angry with me for not believing the truth?'

'Partly,' she said. 'But mostly it was because I was frightened—frightened of being rushed into a marriage I wasn't yet ready for, frightened most of all of the hidden depths in you that I sensed, but could never touch. You were always so tightly self-controlled—I think I wondered what kind of violence had to be so very severely leashed.'

'Yes,' he said after a long moment. 'Yes. I see.'

'I could have found a kinder way,' she said. 'But I was young and scared and pretty confused by my own feelings. And your apparent lack of them.'

'That, my dear,' he said, with a return to his usual manner, 'was not lack of feeling. It was self-control.'

'I think you had rather too much of that.'

'It slipped badly once. *Were* you frightened of me that night?'

'Terrified,' she admitted, shuddering at the memory.

'You slapped my face. I thought I'd only made you angry.'

She shook her head silently, and he said, 'Jealousy was a new experience for me. I'd never felt so savage in my life.'

She put her left hand to his face, stroking his straight brows, and he caught the gleam of her wedding ring and said, 'You should have let me get you a decent engagement ring.'

'Darling, your taste in engagement rings is disastrous. Even the first one you bought me was a bit . . . extravagant. I was always afraid I might lose it. And then you threw it away like a piece of scrap paper. If you'd kept it you might have saved yourself the expense of buying that beastly replacement you offered me. You really must learn to restrain yourself. . . .'

'You're laughing at me again. Will you ever forgive me for offering you that *bauble,* as you called it?'

'You didn't really think you could bribe me into marriage, did you?'

'I suppose not. All I know is I wanted you on any terms, and that very fact made me furious. I wanted to believe that you were like—other women—because then I might have been able to despise you.'

'I thought you *did*.'

'I tried.' He paused. 'I gave the ring to my mother.'

He would probably never come nearer to telling her what he felt about his mother, and how those feelings had influenced his treatment of Larissa.

'I never wanted you for your money,' she said softly. 'Never.'

'I'm sorry I kept harping on that theme,' he said ruefully. 'You see, I knew I had very few personal attractions—'

'That's not true! And I used to think you were an egoist!'

'Keep talking like that and you could turn me into one.'

His hand was stroking her waist, warm against her skin. She inched closer to him, her fingers running across his chest, and said, 'I don't want to talk.'

His hand stroked upwards, and then back to her hip. 'Are you sleepy?' he asked.

'Not a bit. Are you?'

He laughed and turned, pinning her beneath him in the bed. 'Tell me what you want to do,' he ordered.

'Do I have a choice?'

'Not any more.' His voice was husky with desire, hiding nothing from her.

She touched him gently with her fingers and said, 'What happened to your marvellous self-control?'

'Will I need it?'

Wordlessly, she shook her head. He kissed her gently and caressed her until she trembled under him and moved against him yearningly. 'You don't need it,' she whispered urgently. 'You don't need it any more, darling—my darling!'

The floodgates opened again, and carried her high and unprotesting on wave after wave of passion until together they reached the gentle shore on the other side of fulfilled desire, and she saw again the face behind the mask—gentle, loving and almost vulnerable for a few moments before his mouth curved in triumph and his eyes gleamed with pride.

She didn't mind that, and she smiled at him mistily and murmured, 'You're entitled. . . .'

'What?' Tristan whispered, his lips against her hair. But she had already turned her cheek against his shoulder and gone to sleep.

Silhouette Romance

IT'S YOUR OWN SPECIAL TIME

Contemporary romances for today's women.
Each month, six very special love stories will be yours
from SILHOUETTE. Look for them wherever books are sold
or order now from the coupon below.

$1.50 each

Hampson	☐ 1 ☐ 4 ☐ 16 ☐ 27 ☐ 28 ☐ 40 ☐ 52 ☐ 64 ☐ 94	Browning	☐ 12 ☐ 38 ☐ 53 ☐ 73 ☐ 93
Stanford	☐ 6 ☐ 25 ☐ 35 ☐ 46 ☐ 58 ☐ 88	Michaels	☐ 15 ☐ 32 ☐ 61 ☐ 87
		John	☐ 17 ☐ 34 ☐ 57 ☐ 85
Hastings	☐ 13 ☐ 26 ☐ 44 ☐ 67	Beckman	☐ 8 ☐ 37 ☐ 54 ☐ 72 ☐ 96
Vitek	☐ 33 ☐ 47 ☐ 66 ☐ 84		

$1.50 each

☐ 3 Powers	☐ 29 Wildman	☐ 56 Trent	☐ 79 Halldorson
☐ 5 Goforth	☐ 30 Dixon	☐ 59 Vernon	☐ 80 Stephens
☐ 7 Lewis	☐ 31 Halldorson	☐ 60 Hill	☐ 81 Roberts
☐ 9 Wilson	☐ 36 McKay	☐ 62 Hallston	☐ 82 Dailey
☐ 10 Caine	☐ 39 Sinclair	☐ 63 Brent	☐ 83 Hallston
☐ 11 Vernon	☐ 41 Owen	☐ 69 St. George	☐ 86 Adams
☐ 14 Oliver	☐ 42 Powers	☐ 70 Afton Bonds	☐ 89 James
☐ 19 Thornton	☐ 43 Robb	☐ 71 Ripy	☐ 90 Major
☐ 20 Fulford	☐ 45 Carroll	☐ 74 Trent	☐ 92 McKay
☐ 21 Richards	☐ 48 Wildman	☐ 75 Carroll	☐ 95 Wisdom
☐ 22 Stephens	☐ 49 Wisdom	☐ 76 Hardy	☐ 97 Clay
☐ 23 Edwards	☐ 50 Scott	☐ 77 Cork	☐ 98 St. George
☐ 24 Healy	☐ 55 Ladame	☐ 78 Oliver	☐ 99 Camp

$1.75 each

☐ 100 Stanford	☐ 104 Vitek	☐ 108 Hampson	☐ 112 Stanford
☐ 101 Hardy	☐ 105 Eden	☐ 109 Vernon	☐ 113 Browning
☐ 102 Hastings	☐ 106 Dailey	☐ 110 Trent	☐ 114 Michaels
☐ 103 Cork	☐ 107 Bright	☐ 111 South	☐ 115 John
	☐ 116 Lindley	☐ 117 Scott	

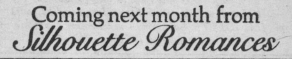

Silhouette ❤ *Romance*

15-Day Free Trial Offer
6 Silhouette Romances

6 Silhouette Romances, free for 15 days! We'll send you 6 new Silhouette Romances to keep for 15 days, absolutely free! If you decide not to keep them, send them back to us. You pay nothing.

Free Home Delivery. But if you enjoy them as much as we think you will, keep them by paying the invoice enclosed with your free trial shipment. We'll pay all shipping and handling charges. You get the convenience of Home Delivery and we pay the postage and handling charge each month.

Don't miss a copy. The Silhouette Book Club is the way to make sure you'll be able to receive every new romance we publish before they're sold out. There is no minimum number of books to buy and you can cancel at any time.